Head-on collision

Allison bent down to retrieve the mail, but Meade did the same, and their heads collided.

"I'm sorry," he muttered.

They stood in silence for a moment, inches apart, gazes locked. Then Meade's brown eyes began to glow with unmistakable desire. Allison caught her breath but didn't move when he leaned forward, touching his lips to hers.

"What was that for?" she blurted out, astounded by the impact of the brief contact.

"I was kissing away the hurt," he explained.

"We bumped *heads*."

"So we did," he agreed, his gaze never leaving her lips. "Want me to get that, too?"

Dear Reader:

Happy July! It's a month for warm summer evenings, barbecues and—of course—the Fourth of July. It's a time of enjoyment and family gatherings. It's a time for romance!

The fireworks are sparkling this month at Silhouette Romance. Our DIAMOND JUBILEE title is *Borrowed Baby* by Marie Ferrarella, a heartwarming story about a brooding loner who suddenly becomes a father when his sister leaves him with a little bundle of joy! Then, next month, don't miss *Virgin Territory* by Suzanne Carey. Dedicated bachelor Phil Catterini is determined to protect the virtue of Crista O'Malley—and she's just as determined to change her status as "the last virgin in Chicago." Looks like his bachelorhood will need the protection instead as these two lovers go hand in hand into virgin territory.

The DIAMOND JUBILEE—Silhouette Romance's tenth anniversary celebration—is our way of saying thanks to you, our readers. To symbolize the timelessness of love, as well as the modern gift of the tenth anniversary, we're presenting readers with a DIAMOND JUBILEE Silhouette Romance title each month, penned by one of your favorite Silhouette Romance authors. In the coming months, writers such as Annette Broadrick, Lucy Gordon, Dixie Browning and Phyllis Halldorson are writing DIAMOND JUBILEE titles especially for you.

And that's not all! There are six books a month from Silhouette Romance—stories by wonderful authors who time and time again bring home the magic of love. During our anniversary year, each book is special and written with romance in mind. July brings you *Venus de Molly* by Peggy Webb—a sequel to her heartwarming *Harvey's Missing*. The second book in Laurie Paige's poignant duo, *Homeward Bound*, is coming your way in July. Don't miss *Home Fires Burning Bright*—Carson and Tess's story. And much-loved Diana Palmer has some special treats in store in the month ahead. Don't miss Diana's fortieth Silhouette—*Connal*. He's a LONG, TALL TEXAN out to lasso your heart, and he'll be available in August....

I hope you'll enjoy this book and all of the stories to come. Come home to romance—Silhouette Romance—for always!

Sincerely,

Tara Hughes Gavin
Senior Editor

LINDA VARNER

Better to Have Loved

Silhouette Romance

Published by Silhouette Books New York

America's Publisher of Contemporary Romance

To Faye and Vick Palmer, parents of my favorite coach
and the best in-laws a romance writer could ever have.

And to Joyce Smith, the kind of friend who doesn't think you're
weird if you brainstorm a new book on the parking lot
of Wal-Mart, and will even add a plot twist or two of her own.

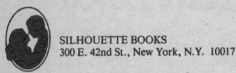

SILHOUETTE BOOKS
300 E. 42nd St., New York, N.Y. 10017

ISBN: 0-373-08734-9

First Silhouette Books printing July 1990

Printed in the U.S.A.

Books by Linda Varner

Silhouette Romance

Heart of the Matter #625
Heart Rustler #644
The Luck of the Irish #665
Honeymoon Hideaway #698
Better to Have Loved #734

LINDA VARNER

has always had a vivid imagination. For that reason, while most people counted sheep to get to sleep, she made up romances. The search for a happy ending sometimes took more than one night, and when some story grew to mammoth proportions, Linda decided to write it down. The result was her first romance novel.

Happily married to her junior high school sweetheart, the mother of two, and a full-time secretary, Linda still finds that the best time to plot her latest project is late at night when the house is quiet and she can create without interruption. Linda lives in Conway, Arkansas, where she was raised, and believes the support of her family, friends, and writers' group made her dream to be published come true.

Allison's Fancy Cream Pie

1 small pkg. gelatin (¼ oz.)
3 tablespoons cold water
3 eggs, separated
½ cup sugar
pinch salt
¼ teaspoon nutmeg
1½ cups milk
½ teaspoon vanilla
1 9" baked pie shell
1 cup whipped cream
¼ cup grated German chocolate

Soak gelatin in cold water for 5 minutes.

Beat egg yolks with sugar, salt and nutmeg. Add milk. Cook in a double boiler over hot, not boiling, water until thickened. Remove from heat, stir in dissolved gelatin, add vanilla and chill until partially set.

Beat egg whites until stiff and add to egg yolk mixture. Pour into pie shell and chill until fully set. Top with whipped cream. Sprinkle with grated chocolate.

Chapter One

Merlin, I need a man, and I need him now," Allison Kendall said. "How about conjuring up a healthy, willing one?"

The sleek black feline blinked opalescent green eyes in answer and then put his tongue to a paw, resuming his toilette.

"Lazy cat," Allison grumbled, tossing her auburn hair over her shoulders and out of her face. "I wasn't going to keep him. I just wanted to borrow his back for a minute so I wouldn't break mine."

Planting her feet firmly on the hardwood floor, she grasped the rolltop desk yet again and pushed with all her might, scooting it a scant two inches nearer its destination, a far wall of the living room. She snorted with impatience, then tried again, grunting and groaning with the effort, yet gaining nothing more than another half inch.

Huffing with exhaustion after two hours of rearranging her second-story, three-room apartment, Allison stomped her foot in exasperation and limped over to the couch. She flopped down on it with a big sigh. Not for the first time that May Saturday morning, Allison wondered what had possessed her to take on the project of moving the beautiful antique now sitting square in the middle of the room surrounded by the drawers that she had taken out of it.

She really knew the reason, of course: habit. Allison Kendall preferred to fly solo.

How she longed to settle herself in the oversize rocker and watch the movie she had received free with the purchase of the portable color television set, stand and videocassette recorder sitting out in her car. Unfortunately she couldn't do that until she finished womanhandling the antique furniture to make room for them—a feat that might not be accomplished in this lifetime from the look of things.

Allison drew a ragged breath and absently petted the cat who had adopted her when she moved into the apartment. She frowned at the heavy desk; it was unbelievably sturdy and twice as heavy as she had anticipated. The fact that she had already moved the love seat, coffee table, rocker *and* bookshelf—each to the accompaniment of multiple bumps and thuds—and was worn out merely increased the difficulty of her task. Allison wished she had, just this once, arranged for some help.

"But who?" she mused aloud. Daisy Rinehart, the owner of the house, might be shockingly spry for seventy-five, but hardly up to this kind of torture. And even after eight months of living in Memphis, Tennessee, Allison knew no one else—male or female—well enough to ask for assistance.

"Come on, wiz," she coaxed, letting her hand brush down the purring cat's back clear to the tip of his tail, which she playfully tweaked. "Do your stuff. He needs to be at least six foot four, two fifty, solid muscle..." Allison laughed softly and closed her eyes, caught up in her fanciful request. "Brown hair, brown eyes, dimples—"

A loud knock rattled her front door and her wits. She jumped in alarm, then darted a nervous glance at Merlin. Surely he hadn't . . . ? But of course not. He was just a cat, after all, and, in spite of his name, had no magical powers. It was probably Daisy, already back from her weekly foray into town and upstairs to see what all the racket was about.

Wearily Allison got to her feet, maneuvering her way to the door through the obstacle course her living room had become. Halfway there another knock sounded and then several more in quick succession, all of them reverberating offensively through the room. In her haste to answer, Allison caught her little toe on the leg of the coffee table that had not been anywhere near that spot twenty minutes earlier.

"Oww!" she exclaimed, hopping in place on her uninjured foot while she caught hold of the other to assess the damage. Tears of sheer agony filled her eyes, momentarily blinding her. Allison blinked them back and took several deep breaths, just as another series of heavy blows rained on the door. Suddenly she saw red.

"I'm coming!" she yelled at the top of her lungs, dead certain it was not the sweet little old widow who lived downstairs.

Ignoring her throbbing toe, Allison stalked the remaining distance to the door, ready to blast whoever stood on the other side. She threw it open wide and saw red again— bright red—on a T-shirt stretched over a male chest worthy of a phone call to the folks at *Guinness Book of World Records*. Biting back the angry words ready to tumble off her tongue, Allison slowly raised her gaze, taking note of the muscled neck, full beard and glinting brown eyes of the very tall stranger before her.

"What in the hell are you doing in here, lady?" he demanded. "You're shaking the whole damn house." He peered over the top of her head into her apartment.

Stunned, Allison had no reply. Her ever-widening stare dropped downward again, missing not one awe-inspiring millimeter of his broad shoulders, powerful arms. She gulped in appreciation, then let her gaze drop past his navy-blue tennis shorts to legs, solid as tree trunks, and jogging shoes Merlin could call home.

Beside the shoes sat the cat, looking guilelessly up at her. Allison looked from her pet to her visitor, then back to her pet. Through the eddy of probabilities and possibilities whirling inside her brain, one rational thought surfaced.

Way to go, Merlin!

"What . . . are . . . you . . . doing . . . in . . . here?" the man repeated, louder this time and enunciating each word with infinite care, as though he thought she might be hard of hearing or maybe an idiot.

Allison was neither.

"Who's asking?" she demanded, placing her hands on her hips and glaring at this muscle-bound man the cat had somehow summoned.

"A man who's been driving all night and needs some sleep, that's who," he growled.

"In *this* house?" Allison blurted, her anger now replaced by shock. The only other occupant of this stately structure was her landlady.

"That's right," he said. "In the apartment down under this one. I'm Meade Duran, Daisy Rinehart's nephew."

Her jaw dropped. "*You're* Meade Duran? *Little* Meade Duran?" Daisy had only mentioned the annual summer visit of her great-nephew a time or two, never once giving Allison any reason to expect an adult, much less such a bear of a man.

He threw his head back and laughed. "Is that what she calls me?"

Allison's face flamed. She nodded numbly.

"Well, I was only ten and the runt of the litter when we met for the first time." He shook his head and grinned. "I guess she still thinks of me that way."

Somehow Allison wasn't surprised by that. Surrounded by antiques and old family photos, Daisy often seemed lost in memories of days gone by.

"I'm Allison Kendall, the renter," Allison said, recovering enough to remember the social skills she taught five days a week. "It's a pleasure to meet you, even if you're not exactly what I expected."

He took the hand she now extended to him, giving it a surprisingly gentle but firm shake before releasing it. "So you thought I was going to be a kid. Disappointed?"

Not sure how to answer that loaded question, Allison hesitated a fraction before candidly replying, "No. Not that I don't love kids, you understand. I do. But they can sure be hard to live with when they're not your own. They get into everything and make a racket." She gave him a rueful smile. "Speaking of which, I guess I owe you an apology for keeping you awake. I had no idea you were in the house."

"No harm done," he said. "But I'd still like to know what you were doing up here." Once again he peered into her apartment. Allison could just imagine what he thought of the mess he saw there.

"Rearranging some furniture," she replied somewhat defensively. "And if I don't get busy, you're never going to get your nap."

"Your husband's helping you?"

"No husband," Allison said coolly to discourage further personal questions.

"Roommate?"

"I live alone," she told him through gritted teeth.

"You were actually moving that desk all by yourself?" he asked next, his dark brows knitted together in a frown.

Feeling as though she'd had her hands slapped, Allison bristled. "I'm stronger than I look."

"Sure you are," he said, pushing past to stride inside. Dumbfounded, Allison hurried after Meade, throwing herself between him and the desk. He set her aside without ceremony, then reached out to test its weight by lifting one corner a couple of inches off the floor. He gave her a hard look. "Trying to kill yourself?"

"Of course not," she responded, by now good and angry at his high-handed tactics.

"Where do you want this?" he then demanded with a speculative perusal of the living room.

Allison hesitated, caught between lifelong, hard-earned independence and her disgusting need for his help. "I really can manage."

Meade gave that lie the attention deserved. "By the window? The door? Speak up, woman. I'm not leaving until you tell me."

Though tempted to tell her landlady's bossy relative a lot more than that, Allison didn't dare. She wouldn't risk hurting that dear old woman's feelings for the world, even if it meant humoring Meade. Besides, she *had* asked for his strong back. Why send him packing without making use of it? Swallowing back her retort with a gulp, Allison murmured, "The window."

Meade caught hold of the desk again, setting himself to the task of sliding it over the floor to the east wall. His muscles rippled with every move and visions of the proverbial bull in the china shop filled Allison's head. She realized that Meade looked sorely out of place in this dainty room adorned with the velvet, brocade and lace of another century.

"How's that?" he asked, turning to face her a moment later.

Allison stepped back to get some perspective and winced. The desk didn't look nearly as good there as she had hoped. "Can we try over by the door?"

Without a word, Meade moved the desk. He turned to face her again, one eyebrow arched in silent inquiry.

Allison cocked her head, studying the new arrangement, the papered wall and the door. Something still wasn't right. "How about another couple of feet to the left?"

Again Meade complied with her request. "Better?"

"Worse," she said with a sigh of frustration.

"How about over in that corner?" Meade suggested.

"Actually, that's where it came from," Allison replied. She pivoted, scanning the room for a better spot for the massive piece of furniture. Maybe if she switched the love seat and the desk and then moved the bookshelf... "Uh, just how sleepy *are* you?"

It was Meade's turn to sigh. "Got any coffee?"

"I don't drink the nasty stuff myself," Allison told him. "But Daisy keeps a fresh pot all the time. I'll run down and get you some."

"First tell me what you want where," he said, clearly resigned to whatever lay ahead.

Allison did just that—in minute detail—and then hurried to the door. Before she exited, she stopped and whirled back around to face him. "How do you take your coffee?"

Meade looked around the room, obviously assessing the size of his task. "Better make it black," he said, moving with determined strides to the love seat.

Since Allison wanted to supervise his endeavors, she dashed downstairs to the kitchen and the coffee maker. But there was no hot coffee ready and waiting this sunny morning. There wasn't even any cold coffee she could heat up in the microwave oven. In fact, the coffeepot sat in the dish drainer, upside down.

Allison groaned in dismay, wondering why today of all days Daisy had made a break with tradition. Hurriedly she sidestepped Guinevere and Lancelot, Merlin's golden-haired siblings, to head to the pantry she and Daisy shared. She borrowed a can of coffee from one of the shelves on Daisy's side and followed the measuring instructions on the side of it. Then, with a flick of the wrist, she turned on the coffee maker just as someone banged on the back door. Muttering her disgust with unwanted intrusions, Allison walked to the curtained door to open it.

"Where's Daisy?" immediately demanded a rotund man she recognized as Quincy Luther from the house next door.

"She's out," Allison told him, eyeing the tiger-striped cat he clutched. Yet another member of Daisy's round table of felines, this mischievous sibling was named Arthur.

"Well, I need to talk to her. *Now.*"

"She's out," Allison coolly repeated. She had never cared much for Mr. Luther.

Quincy snorted his impatience and thrust Arthur at Allison. "You tell that old woman to keep her damn cats out of my yard. This one was trying to get in my bluebird box and I won't have it!"

"You'd better speak to Daisy yourself," Allison, who made a study of minding her own business, replied. "I'm sure she'll be back in an hour or two."

At that she stepped back and firmly shut the door, cutting off his outraged "Hmmpf!" with pleasure.

"Naughty cat," Allison then scolded halfheartedly, setting Arthur on the floor with his brother and sister. Sniff-
ing the heavenly scent now filling the kitchen, she walked
back to the counter. How could anything that smelled so
wonderful taste so bad? she wondered for the umpteenth
time, reaching for one of the white ceramic mugs dangling
from hooks in the cabinet.

Just over twenty minutes after Allison entered the
kitchen, she left it to head upstairs, full mug in hand. She
opened her door, halting abruptly at the sight that greeted
her. Every piece of furniture had been arranged as requested and Meade Duran now lay stretched out on her love
seat, snoring softly, his legs dangling over an armrest.

"Oh no," she moaned in disbelief, crossing the room and
setting the coffee on the side table. She glared at Meade.

Though easy on the eyes, his considerable breadth and
height were rather intimidating. Why, he probably outweighed her a good hundred pounds, if not more, and
topped her five foot nine by at least eight inches. In her
whole twenty-seven years, Allison had never met anyone
quite this size. She was awed.

The bright red letters on his T-shirt told her he was on the
staff at McCallister Boys' School in Atlanta, Georgia. Has
to be a coach, she decided. But what kind? She almost
wished she had accepted one of Daisy's countless invita-
tions to tea and the "nice little chat" that probably would
have revealed all she could possibly want to know—and
more—about this man.

But an afternoon tête-à-tête was out of the question, of
course. What if Daisy grew too attached, suggested they
take their meals together or go shopping? Allison wanted
no part of any misguided mothering. She had worked too
hard to establish her independence and, at this point of her

life, didn't need a husband, family or even friends to
threaten the norm.

She didn't need a bossy Meade Duran, either, and put
out a hand to wake and get rid of him. At that moment he
stirred slightly, annihilating her composure. Allison jerked
back her hand and placed it on her thumping heart in an
attempt to calm it. Then she laughed nervously at her reaction and reached out again.

But she just couldn't touch him. Why? she wondered,
letting her hand fall limply to her side and edging away to
the safety of the rocker to assess the situation. Was it his
muscles that intimidated her? The luxuriant hair and
beard? Or the fact that he was a heartbreak waiting to
happen?

All of the above, she decided, not to mention the
months—no, years she'd endured without male companionship. Why else would she be acting like such a ninny?
Why else would her pulse rate be in triple digits? Her palms
sweaty? Meade was a shock to her self-imposed celibacy.
The sooner she chased him back downstairs, the better.

And until then, Allison had plenty of work to keep her
mind occupied. She stood and perused the room, smiling
at what she saw. It looked great. Perfect. Now all she had
to do was put the drawers back in the desk, the books back
on the shelves and the oriental rug back on the floor. Surely
by that time Meade would be awake. Surely.

Actually he was awake long before that, wide-awake and
watching Allison's every move through half-closed lids. His
gaze swept her red shorts and white T-shirt before settling
on long, bare legs and a temptingly rounded bottom. He
shifted his attention front and topside to full breasts, slender arms and a very attractive oval face. There he lingered,
noting big brown eyes, flushed cheeks and the kind of
mouth that could drive a man right out of his mind. Not

bad, he thought, mentally nodding his approval. Very graceful. Every inch a lady.

Since most of Meade's one-on-one dealings lately had involved women who were not, he found Allison fascinating. What had Daisy told him about her? he wondered, trying to remember past conversations with the spry old woman. He could think of nothing but her comment that Allison always paid her rent on time. To that "punctual" he could now add "single" and "shapely"—qualities that were not only important, but also served to increase his rabid curiosity about her.

Deliberately Meade stirred and then stretched with what he hoped were the lazy movements of a man just waking from deep slumber. Unfortunately Merlin chose that moment to pounce on Meade's flat belly, claws extended for the kill. Oscar performance duly demolished, Meade scrambled to his feet with a yelp of surprise.

"You're awake," Allison said, immediately grabbing the coffee mug and thrusting it at him.

"Yeah," he muttered, taking it. "Sorry about that nap."

"It's okay," she said. "I know you must be beat and I won't keep you a moment longer. Thanks so much for your help." Obviously anxious to be rid of him, she moved to the door and opened it. But Meade wasn't quite ready to leave. He had several dozen questions he wanted answered first.

Sipping the coffee, now lukewarm and black with a capital *B*, he ignored her, taking a seat in the platform rocker instead. "Thanks. This is, uh, stimulating. Just what I needed." Meade forced himself to take another swallow and then smiled at her, hoping to erase the sudden look of wariness from her eyes. "How do you like living here?"

"Fine," she said, not budging from where she stood by the open door.

"Good, good." He took another sip. "Where are you from?"

Allison hesitated before she replied. "Nashville."

"Nashville, huh? I've never been there." He waited for her to take up the slack in the conversation, but she didn't, and the silence grew awkward before he tried again. "I'm from Australia, myself. A little town just north of Sydney. Ever been down under?"

"No."

Another weighty quiet followed that brief reply and Meade acknowledged that most men with social savvy or an ounce of tact would give up and go. He had neither, and years of coaching rebellious teenagers had taught him that persistence always paid off—in the gym or in a woman's apartment. Maybe if he abandoned the direct approach she would relax and open up a little.

"It's a beautiful country. We've got mountains, deserts, beaches—something for everyone. I go back to visit as often as I can," he added, certain she would now speak up and sing the glories of *her* hometown.

But she didn't. So he gave up that topic of discussion and changed the subject. "Isn't Daisy great? She's been more like a grandmother than an aunt to me. Always had a plate of cookies, a glass of milk and some sound advice waiting when I got in a jam. She was the one who talked me into trying karate as a means of working off some of my teenage frustrations. It has really paid off for me."

"I see," she said.

He realized she really didn't and explained, "Karate is my life and my living. I teach it at a boys' school. Do you know anything about the martial arts?"

Allison shrugged. "Very little, and what I've seen on television and in the movies looks much too violent for my tastes."

"I see," he said, and *he* did. Put firmly in his place, Meade gave up with good grace and got to his feet. There would be other—better—times to get to know Allison Kendall. He was going to be in Memphis for two weeks, after all. "Guess I'd better go...unless you need me for something else?" He flashed her the last-resort, killer smile he saved for desperate situations.

She wasn't impressed. "Not a thing," she told him, adding, "Thanks again for your help," as she moved back so he could exit.

"Don't mention it," he glumly replied, stepping into the carpeted hallway. The closing door brushed his heels and bruised what remained of his ego. Shaking his head in disgust, Meade descended the stairs to Daisy's apartment and her horde of cats, none of whom interested him half as much as Allison did.

Chapter Two

It took Allison ten whole minutes to get up the nerve to open the door again and peek out into the hallway. After verifying that Meade had indeed moved on, she tiptoed to the balustrade to peer down into the parquet entranceway of the old house. There was no sign of him there, either.

Sighing her relief, Allison carefully made her way down the steps. She kept to the edges so the aged wood wouldn't creak and give her away, then sighed again when she made it to the front door undetected. So far, so good. Ever so quietly, Allison walked out onto the sunlit porch, only then allowing herself a grin of victory.

A short flight of stairs and a brick sidewalk later found her slipping between her little sedan and the vintage hardtop now parked beside it. She eyed the sleek vehicle—obviously Meade's—with admiration, then turned to the business of opening her trunk and tugging the boxed television out. Though a bundle, it was manageable, and she foresaw no problems in carrying it up to her apartment.

Seconds after puffing her way back onto the porch and maneuvering open the screen door, Allison modified her assessment. Clearly this little task wasn't going to be quite as easy as she'd hoped. Her arms had begun to ache, like her already weary back, and she still had a flight of stairs to go.

Supporting her load on one knee, Allison readjusted her grip and then plunged on and upward, managing to ascend halfway before the smooth pasteboard box began to slip out of her fingers. Vainly she tried to reposition her hands, but it was too late.

The box continued its downward slide, painfully scraping the skin off one bare shin as it thudded to the steps. Allison froze, listening and waiting for Daisy's guest to spring forth and nab her. But he didn't, and she released her pent-up breath in a whoosh of gratitude before turning her attention back to her task.

Allison bent down to grasp the box and then put every muscle to the test, stretching, straining and finally lifting.

"Holy mackerel, woman!" Meade's rich baritone rang out just as she straightened. Startled out of her wits, Allison lost her grip on the box, which crashed once again to the steps.

"Didn't anyone ever teach you the right way to pick up something as big as this?" Meade demanded, loping up the stairs to join Allison. He reached for the box, now balanced precariously on the step. "You're supposed to use your knees, not your back," he scolded, adding, "Like this," as he demonstrated proper technique.

"Thank you, *coach*," Allison muttered with ill grace, reaching out to relieve him of his burden.

But Meade shook his head. "I'll get this. You get the door."

Allison didn't even bother to argue with him. She knew it would do no good. Instead, taking the steps two at a time, she hurried on up to push open the door of her apartment so he could enter. Meade walked in and set the box on the coffee table before straightening to peruse the recently rearranged room.

"Where were you going to put this?" he asked, frowning slightly.

"Over there," Allison told him. "On my new TV stand."

He glanced in that direction, noting the empty corner. "What stand?"

Allison hesitated before reluctantly admitting, "The one still out in the car in a box. I'll have to put it together first."

"Got any tools?"

"According to the man who sold it to me, all I'll need is a flat-head screwdriver," she said. "I do have one of those."

"Go get it. I'll get the stand and assemble it for you," he told her, exiting the apartment so quickly he didn't hear her immediate protest. Merlin was not so lucky.

"I'm perfectly capable of putting together four lousy pieces of wood," Allison snapped to the feline as she headed dutifully to the bedroom closet and the old metal box where she kept such essentials as a hammer, screwdrivers, nails and pliers. She considered herself pretty darn good with tools and resented Meade's assumption that, being female, she naturally required his help.

Temper simmering, Allison was waiting for Meade when he stepped back into the room, TV stand tucked under one powerful arm, videocassette recorder under the other. She held her peace until he'd set the boxes on the floor, then opened her mouth to thank him for his efforts thus far and send him on his way.

"I assume you wanted the VCR up here, too?" he asked, before she could utter a word.

"Well, yes, but—"

"Find the screwdriver?"

"Yes, but—"

"Good." He reached out for the screwdriver she still clutched, arching one eyebrow in surprise when she tightened her grip on it and refused to give it to him.

"You've done enough," Allison stated flatly. "I appreciate it, but I can manage alone from here."

"Nonsense," Meade said, giving the screwdriver a firm tug that freed it from her fingers. "I'm more than willing to help out, and while I'm at it, I'll hook up your TV and VCR, too."

"But—"

"No buts. Glad to do it."

Allison threw her hands up in defeat. Clearly she had lost control of the situation. And since she was too much of a lady to yell, "Beat it, buster!" she had no option but to let him have his way. "Is there anything I can do to help?"

"As a matter of fact there is," he said, reaching for his almost full mug, which he handed to her. "I'm afraid my coffee has gotten cold. Would you mind...?"

Allison did mind—a lot. Especially since she suspected the request was nothing more than a ploy to get her out from underfoot.

What he needs is a good punch in the nose, she thought, a decidedly unladylike idea that nonetheless appealed greatly. At that moment, Meade reached for the boxed television stand, a movement that produced rippling back muscles and bulging biceps. Allison gulped at the sight and abruptly abandoned all notions of violence. Turning on her heel, she stalked down the stairs to fetch the coffee. When she returned minutes later, it was to find that Meade had already assembled the stand and was now attempting to lift the television free of its thick foam packing and the box. Tightly wedged, it didn't want to budge.

"Need some help?" she asked, rather pleased that even macho men sometimes had their problems.

"Grab that flap there."

What's the magic word? Allison wanted to prompt as she often did young students. She said nothing, however, since she felt certain Meade had never said *please* in his life. Setting down the mug, she silently moved to assist him.

When the empty box had been tossed out of the way and the television placed on its stand, Meade took a sip of his coffee, gave Allison a "thumbs-up" and set to work unpacking the VCR. Ten minutes later, he turned on the television, now hooked up to the VCR and the cable line installed the day before. The screen lit up with a colorful, wonderfully clear picture, quite a change from the blurry black-and-white reception Allison had tolerated for the past three years.

"I think that does it," Meade commented. "Do you have a tape we can use to test the recorder?"

"Just some blanks," Allison told him. "And the movie they gave me free with purchase."

"Yeah? Which one?"

"The African Queen."

"Bogart and Hepburn! My favorites. Let's watch it," Meade said with a grin of delight. He walked over to the love seat, plopped down and reached for his coffee, looking for all the world like a man prepared to stay forever. Allison panicked.

"I really don't think—" she began, just as someone called Meade's name from downstairs. Recognizing her landlady's voice, Allison sighed with relief. "I believe I hear Daisy calling you."

"Is she back already?" Meade got to his feet and walked to the open door to peer downstairs. "I'll be right down," he called out. Then he turned to Allison. "Looks like she bought a bunch of groceries, and after telling me she didn't need any. I guess I'd better go help with them."

Oh so thankful he'd focused his gallantry on someone else, Allison quickly nodded her assent. "I'm sure she'd appreciate it," she said, belatedly adding, "Thanks for all your help."

"No problem," he told her, stepping out into the hall. Allison walked to the door to shut Meade out of her apartment. Before she managed that simple task, however, Daisy called out to her.

"Allison?"

She pretended she hadn't heard and gently pushed on the door.

"Allison?" It was Meade this time.

She winced, sighed and stuck her head out into the hall. "Yes?"

"Can you come down for a moment, dear?" Daisy asked. "I'd like to talk to you."

What now? Allison wondered, reluctantly stepping outside and down the stairs. She and Daisy seldom exchanged more than perfunctory pleasantries, a routine she didn't want to change.

"I see you've met Meade," Daisy said when Allison joined them in the foyer.

"Yes, I have," Allison replied. "He's been a big, uh, help to me this morning."

"Isn't he a dear?" Daisy gushed.

That's one word for it, Allison mentally answered, though aloud she merely murmured, "Isn't he, though?" She glanced at Meade, who peered into the sack he held.

"You told me you had enough food for the weekend," he said to Daisy. "Why'd you bother with these today?"

"I just bought some cat food," the petite woman explained. "The Bargain Market had it on sale and the senior citizens' van drives right by there."

Meade reached inside and pulled out a can of cat food. "Holy mackerel, Daisy," he exclaimed, his narrowed gaze now on the price stamped on the tiny can. "I'll bet those damn cats of yours eat better than you do."

Daisy's naturally rosy cheeks flushed a vivid crimson at his comment. Clearly flustered, she took the can from him and headed for the kitchen. Meade followed one step behind.

Not for the first time that morning, Allison's temper flared. Someone should tell that man to mind his own business, she thought, starting after him to do just that. Then she halted, surprised by her intense desire to defend a woman she liked well enough but didn't want to love.

Maybe it's time to mind my own, she qualified, abruptly pivoting to race back upstairs.

"Allison, wait!"

Allison turned to find Daisy had stepped back out of the kitchen and now stood at the bottom of the steps, one dainty hand on the polished wood banister.

"I want to have a special dinner tonight to welcome Meade," Daisy said. "I was hoping you'd join us."

"Thanks so much, but I have other plans," Allison lied before resuming her climb. She managed to reach the top of the staircase before Meade caught her elbow in an iron grip.

"Can't you cancel them?" he asked, stepping up beside her on the landing. "It's Daisy's birthday, you know. And it'd really mean a lot to her if you came to her party."

Daisy's birthday? Allison hadn't known.

"It's the least you can do," Meade softly prompted, as though sensing her indecision. "After all, she adores you."

Adores me?

"Please?"

The magic word, Allison sighed. Not for anything would she hurt Daisy Rinehart's feelings . . . even if she had to endure an evening of Meade Duran.

"Oh, all right," she said. "But only if I bring dessert and can have two hours *alone* in the kitchen to prepare it."

Meade grinned his triumph. "I can arrange that," he promised.

Allison never doubted for a moment that he could.

Humming softly to herself, Allison entered the kitchen a few hours later, two sacks of groceries in hand. She glanced at the wall clock. Only one-fifteen, she realized. Plenty of time left before dinner to create her masterpiece.

As Meade had promised, she was alone in the surprisingly modern room, except for a cat or two. Sidestepping a particularly affectionate one, Allison unloaded her groceries, lining up the items she would need to stir up what she hoped would be the most beautiful birthday cake Daisy had ever seen. In reality, Allison had her doubts.

Though adept at baking and decorating cakes of every shape and size, Allison hadn't practiced the art in almost a year—since she quit working as a wedding consultant to a florist and started her own business in Memphis. As owner of Etiquette, Etc., her consultant talents now included not only weddings, but business etiquette, home entertaining, telephone manners and whatever else her clients might request. She had no time to bake anymore and, happily, no longer needed the additional income her confections had once provided.

Allison retrieved a box from the pantry and extracted a well-worn cookbook, two cake pans and decorating paraphernalia. Her confidence in her baking abilities returned as she measured ingredients. Soon Allison found herself humming again.

In no time the cake was in the oven and Allison stood at the sink, washing the mixing bowl and beaters. She relished the peace of the moment and the satisfaction always experienced when working in such a well-equipped kitchen as this. Suddenly she wished for a house of her own—a house big enough for two or even more, a house made for laughter and love.

Now where did that come from? Allison wondered, sighing her impatience at such foolishness. Years ago she had decided she was meant for a business career and not marriage. There was a divorce decree tucked away in a file upstairs to remind her why.

Besides, she was happy with her role as spinster.

"Make that bachelorette," she qualified aloud, grimacing at the sound of that neologism. Bachelorette or spinster, the bottom line was the same: Allison Kendall was going to spend the rest of her life single.

Thank goodness that was how she really wanted it.

"Something sure smells good," a very familiar voice commented from the doorway a good half hour later.

Allison flipped over the cake pan she held, turning the last golden-brown layer out onto the cooling rack before whirling to confront Meade, who lounged negligently against the doorjamb, all smiles.

"You promised I'd have the kitchen to myself," she curtly reminded him.

"And you will," he said. "Just as soon as I get Daisy a cup of tea. She wanted to make it herself, but I wouldn't let her come in." Whistling off-key, he walked to the cup-

board. There he opened and shut each and every door until he found a china cup and saucer, which he set out on the
counter. Then he rummaged noisily through the pictur-
esque tins of tea Daisy kept in a row on top of the refrigerator. "Which does she like best?" he asked without
turning around, weighing a tin in each hand. "Spiced or
mint?"

"Hmm?" Allison murmured, more distracted by the
view of his nicely rounded back pockets and long muscled
legs than her task of measuring confectioners' sugar into a
bowl.

"What kind of tea does Daisy prefer?" Meade asked,
unexpectedly pivoting to face her.

"Oh, uh, I really couldn't say," Allison stammered,
hoping he hadn't caught her staring at his tush. Hastily she
stirred margarine into the sugar.

"Guess I'll make it mint, then," Meade said. He filled
the cup with water and set it in the microwave, switching the
appliance on before Allison gathered wits enough to stop
him.

"Don't!" she exclaimed, just as a loud pop and a flash
signaled disaster.

Meade jumped in response and frowned his bewilderment. "What the hell was that?"

"You blew a fuse," Allison explained with a sigh.

"I do that a lot," he retorted with a grin any female
would consider charming.

Allison, who wasn't just "any" female and who wasn't
charmed, either, did not smile back. "The microwave can't
be used if anything else is plugged into that outlet, like this
mixer is now," she explained.

"Guess I'd better take a look at it while I'm here. Right
now I'd better replace that fuse. Where's the box?"

Allison led the way to the screened back porch and supervised the insertion of a new fuse from the spares Daisy kept handy. Then she assisted Meade in making the tea so she could hurry him on his way, not an easy task since he seemed to have an inordinate interest in her baking.

Only when he finally left the kitchen, cup in hand, did Allison relax. Regrouping with difficulty, she turned her concentration back to her work, only to lose it again shortly after when Meade strolled into the kitchen once more.

"What do you want now?" she demanded in frustration.

"I want to watch you decorate the cake," he said.

He wanted to watch? Baffled by this unexpected display of little-boy curiosity from such a giant of a man, Allison didn't quite know how to respond. "I...um...there's really nothing to it...."

"Looks pretty complicated to me," Meade argued, softly adding, "Please?"

And she'd thought he didn't know how to use the word. "I guess you can watch, but you have to promise not to talk to me or touch anything."

"I promise," Meade said solemnly, turning a chair around backward so he could straddle it. He crossed his arms over the back, rested his chin on them and waited expectantly.

Allison dragged her eyes away with effort. She stared blankly at the bowl of fluffy white frosting, for a moment at a loss for just what she'd planned to do with it. Then, huffing her disgust with herself, she snatched up a spatula.

"What are you going to do?" Meade asked, then hastily mumbled, "Sorry, sorry," when she immediately glared at him.

Relishing the heavy silence that ensued, Allison worked quickly to stack the layers and ice the entire cake. Then, using a decorator bag and tube, she rimmed each layer with a lacy edging of tinted frosting.

"That's amazing," Meade muttered under his breath. "Just amazing."

Strangely warmed by his praise, Allison didn't scold him. Instead she handed over the bowl she'd just emptied so he could scrape it clean.

Surprised and oddly touched by the offering, Meade took it with pleasure. He hadn't cleaned a frosting bowl in years and didn't intend to leave one single swirl of the sweet now. "Mmm, thanks. Where did you learn to do this?"

"College," she told him. "Home ec major."

"You ever thought about teaching it?" he asked.

"I already teach. Sort of," she replied. "I'm an etiquette consultant."

"You mean like Emily Post or Gloria Vanderbilt?"

Allison laughed at that, making a magical sound Meade hadn't heard before. Her smile transformed her face from pretty to beautiful, and his heart turned over in response.

"It's *Amy* Vanderbilt," she told him, "and I guess my job is similar to theirs. I have an office a few blocks south of here where I hold classes in social skills."

"For who?" he next asked, highly intrigued. If there was any area in which he was lacking, it was probably social skills. Hadn't more than one girlfriend, not to mention his own mother, hinted that might be so? Still, Allison seemed so cool, so detached; somehow he couldn't picture her in a classroom relating to common man.

"For anyone. I've advised businessmen, beauty queens, preschoolers..." Allison's voice trailed off as she turned her attention back to her task. With awe-inspiring skill, she transformed the cake into a work of art adorned with delicate sugar daisies. Meade rose quietly from his chair and crept closer to watch over her shoulder, fascinated by both her profession and the magic she now worked. Though bursting with questions about her business, he stood in silence until she'd finished writing "Happy Birthday" and positioned a candle shaped like a seventy-six.

"How about a black belt?" he then questioned softly. "Ever try to tame one of those?"

Allison started at the sound of his voice in her ear and spun around to find him towering over her, so close she could actually smell his after-shave. The sinfully masculine scent hypnotized her, lured her. Allison held her breath to keep from inhaling it and edged deliberately away.

"I can't say that I have," she murmured self-consciously before picking up her plastic bowl and tossing it into the sink.

"The cake looks great," Meade said. "I'm impressed, and Daisy will be, too. Now where are you going to hide it until the party?"

"Good question," Allison murmured. She rinsed the bowl, placed it bottom side up in the drainer, then glanced around the room. "How about the top shelf on my side of the pantry. There's nothing on it."

"*Your* side? You two don't share groceries?"

"No. My food is on the left, Daisy's is on the right. Same goes for the refrigerator."

"Oh." Meade took the cake and stepped into the pantry. He set it on the shelf, then turned to her, frowning. "There's hardly anything but cat food on Daisy's side. What does she eat, for Pete's sake?"

"I really don't know," Allison had to admit, washing the spoons and spatula. "We don't dine together."

Meade digested that in silence and then strode over to the refrigerator to jerk open the door.

"Hell, there's nothing in here, either!" he exclaimed, slamming it shut again. "It's a damn good thing we're going to the grocery store Monday." He strode over to where Allison stood and caught her arm, turning her away from the sink full of bubbles to face him. His eyes bored into hers. "Is Daisy doing okay?" he demanded. "Is she well? Happy?"

Allison automatically opened her mouth to reassure him, then shut it again. The man was obviously disturbed about his old aunt and maybe with good reason. He deserved an honest answer.

"Again . . . I don't know. We both stay busy and seldom have a chance to socialize."

Though Meade said nothing, his immediate look of censure told Allison he saw right through that flimsy explanation. She squirmed, realizing she had no good excuse for sequestering herself in her apartment and avoiding a poor old woman who was probably as lonely as she was.

Lonely? Allison Kendall? Of course not, and darn Meade Duran for confusing her! She turned her back on him again, making short work of her cleanup.

"Well, that does it," she murmured seconds later, ill at ease under Meade's accusing gaze. She slipped past him. "I guess I'll see you and Daisy later."

"Dinner's at seven," Meade told Allison as she hurried out the door to the haven of her apartment. "And we *won't* be having cat food."

Chapter Three

Allison's apartment was depressingly quiet that afternoon, not the haven it usually was. She alternately sat and paced until dinnertime, her mind on the mismatched pair downstairs.

Daisy was a dear, a woman who would willingly be a friend and confidante, just as Allison's grandmother had once been. Daisy was also old and wouldn't live forever. Allison well remembered the pain of losing her beloved grandmother even after so many years. She certainly didn't want to experience that kind of heartbreak again, even if Meade thought her cold and unfeeling.

As for *him*, well, there was no doubt in Allison's mind that she should avoid Meade as well. Though sexy as all get-out, he was simply too nosy, too pushy, too...everything. His teasing ways got on her nerves and embarrassed her. The man had no couth. She did not want to be around him, especially if he were going to expect an apology for her solitary way of life.

Promptly at seven, Allison made her way downstairs. She glanced at her coral cotton sundress, wondering yet again if something more casual, like pants, might not have been better. She didn't want Meade to think she'd taken any great pains about getting ready tonight. But then again, she didn't want Daisy to think she hadn't.

Allison found the woman folding linen napkins in the formal dining room. All the extra leaves had been removed from the usually long table so that it was now quite small—too small and intimate to Allison's way of thinking. A lace cloth had been spread, and the table set with what had to be Daisy's best china and silverware. Crystal goblets reflected the glow of lighted tapers in the floral centerpiece. Allison, who loved formal affairs, was suddenly glad she had dressed for the occasion. Clearly Daisy was going all out.

At that moment, Meade entered the dining room from the kitchen door. He carried a huge platter, artfully laden with pot roast and the trimmings. But it wasn't the entrée Allison saw. It was the man.

And what a man.

Dressed in a sport coat, undoubtedly *his* idea of going all out, he looked so tall, so broad, so darn gorgeous—a sight for appreciative female eyes.

It's going to be a long night, Allison immediately decided, a prediction that proved true over the next two hours. Though cooked to a turn and seasoned perfectly, the pot roast had almost no taste to Allison. She found herself moving food around on her plate, barely managing to swallow a bite now and then. Directly across the table from her sat Meade, who didn't have her problem. He cleared his plate with gusto, apparently oblivious to the way his knees and feet bumped hers every time he shifted his long legs.

Allison wasn't so immune, and by dessert time, she'd had enough of that tingling contact, not to mention the chit-chat good manners naturally demanded. She felt like an intruder, a fifth wheel, in spite of an obvious effort on her hostess's part to draw her into the circle of their love. Though somewhere deep inside, Allison envied them that closeness, she steadfastly refused to admit it. Instead she plotted her escape, barely registering Daisy's cry of plea-sure when Meade brought the cake into the room.

"Oh, my dear," the birthday "girl" exclaimed. "You shouldn't have!"

Daisy's dancing blue eyes and sunny smile made Alli-son's efforts worthwhile. She forced herself to relax and suddenly remembered the gift she had picked up on her outing earlier that afternoon. Shyly, she handed Daisy a small beribboned box.

"For me?" Tears swam in the woman's eyes. Allison felt a sharp stab of regret for the friendship she had wasted these eight months, regret she ruthlessly suppressed.

Daisy tore eagerly into the box, exclaiming her delight when she lifted a square of cotton to reveal a gold-and-rhinestone brooch.

"It's just beautiful," she said, immediately pinning it to her dress. To Allison's embarrassment, she then rose from the table to give her a big hug. "Thank you."

"Y-you're welcome," Allison stammered, cheeks flam-ing. Her own eyes stung with threatening tears, a develop-ment that distressed her to no end. Hastily she reached for the cake knife and held it out to Daisy, who had returned to her chair. "You do the honors."

"Wait," Meade interjected from where he stood behind his aunt. "I haven't given her my gift yet, and she hasn't blown out the candle."

Meade's gift turned out to be a handknitted cashmere shawl. Allison had never seen anything quite so elegant. Apparently neither had Daisy, who broke down and cried.

"I'm sorry," she said, once she'd gotten control of herself. "I'm just a sentimental old fool."

"Sentimental, maybe," Meade replied, dropping to his knee beside her chair. He kissed her soundly and smiled. "Old fool? Never."

And Allison had thought him uncouth. Obviously there was more here than met the eye. Why, he might even be a man she could like ... darn the luck.

To Allison's relief, Daisy composed herself enough to blow out her single candle easily. She then cut the cake into generous pieces. Allison barely managed to choke hers down, but again Meade made up for her lack of appetite.

"That was great," he said, after downing the last bite of his second slice. "Well worth the extra miles I'll have to run as penance."

"Meade's really into physical fitness," Daisy told Allison, who'd definitely noticed. "He coaches right now but is going to open a chain of family wellness centers soon."

"If I can get the money I need," Meade interjected, adding, "I'm trying to find financial backing now."

"You're going to give up coaching?" Allison asked.

"Yes," he replied. "It was a difficult decision, but the right one, I think. It's high time for me to branch out, be my own boss."

"Do you think you'll miss working with teenagers?"

"Without a doubt," he admitted. "That's why I intend to continue my weekend karate classes at the Y."

"Meade does other kinds of volunteer work, too," Daisy said. "He and one of the local policemen hold workshops on self-defense and home security." She smiled proudly. "Friday night, he's going to share some common sense safety tips he's learned with my ladies' circle. You can come, if you'd like.''

"Oh, I don't think—'' Allison began, halting her automatic refusal when someone knocked on the back door. Excusing herself, she gratefully volunteered to answer it.

At the door stood Judy Sharp, a woman Allison had met once before and who was the daughter of Daisy's best friend. "Is Daisy home?" she asked, obviously agitated.

Before Allison could summon the older woman, she entered the kitchen. "Why, Judy, do come in. You're just in time for cake."

"I can't," Judy said, shaking her head. "I'm on my way to the hospital. Mama broke her hip this afternoon."

"Oh, no!" Daisy exclaimed. "What happened?"

Hastily the redhead told her, ending with, "You remember those two six-week-old dachshunds I bought for her just last night?"

Daisy nodded.

"Would you take them? Mama simply doesn't need the responsibility right now and I know you have a new pen and a house that you're not using."

"Of course I will," Daisy told her, obviously delighted. Within minutes Judy retrieved the two puppies from her car, handed them over and drove away.

The second she pulled out of the drive, Meade, who had come to the kitchen and apparently caught the last of the conversation, demanded, "What dog pen? What doghouse?"

"I had a house and pen constructed for a dalmatian who wandered in out of the rain a couple of months ago," Daisy, now on her knees soothing the frightened pups, explained. "Unfortunately the poor thing died of distemper before he made use of them. Now isn't it lucky for these two precious puppies that I'm so well prepared?"

Meade said nothing, but Allison thought his frown spoke volumes. To cover the awkward silence following Daisy's explanation, she asked, "What are you going to name them?"

"How about Marian and Robin?" Daisy asked.

Before Allison could voice her opinion, Meade groaned his. "Does that mean you're going to try to fill the pen with 'merry men'? Damn, Daisy. How are you going to feed them all? You've got too many pets as it is."

Before Daisy could respond, Allison, who'd had quite enough of Meade *and* his unwanted interference in their lives, leaped to her landlady's defense. "I don't believe she asked for your opinion."

"At least I care enough about her to have one," Meade retorted. That truth hit home, resurrecting all of Allison's guilt feelings...and her ire.

Drawing on years of experience in handling difficult people, Allison managed to cling to her temper. With remarkable calm, she bid them both a brisk good-night and, turning on her heel, exited the room. She headed automatically for the stairs, then impulsively whirled, detouring to the mailbox on the front porch. Seconds later, sorting the mail she'd found there, Allison stepped back inside. She immediately collided with Meade, who had materialized from nowhere. Envelopes of every color and size sailed in all directions.

With an exclamation of disgust, Allison stepped away from him and bent to retrieve them. But he'd done the same, and this time their heads collided.

"Hell, I'm sorry," he muttered, belatedly adding, "For everything."

Realizing that was probably the most eloquent apology she'd ever receive from him, Allison graciously accepted and offered one of her own. "So am I."

They stood in silence for a moment, inches apart, gazes locked. Then Meade's brown eyes began to glow with unmistakable desire. Allison caught her breath in surprise, but captive of those eyes, didn't move when he leaned forward, touching his lips to hers.

"What was that for?" she blurted, astounded by the impact of that brief, brushing contact. She put a hand out to clutch a nearby table, lending support to her weakened knees.

"I was kissing away the hurt," he explained, clearly as shocked as she by that electrically charged kiss.

Allison drew a steadying breath, determined to keep her cool. "We bumped *heads*."

"So we did," he agreed, his eyes never leaving her lips. "Want me to get that, too?"

Certain she'd collapse into an undignified heap at his feet if he did, Allison hastily shook her head. With hands that shook, she gathered and sorted the mail, haphazardly thrusting Daisy's at him before dashing up the stairs to the safety of her apartment.

Meade watched Allison until she disappeared into her apartment, then winced at the slam of her door.

So much for getting to know the renter better, he thought with a wry grin as he slipped out of the hated jacket. Meade draped it absently over the back of a chair, his mind on how beautiful Allison had looked tonight in that coral dress, how her topaz eyes sparkled. She was one lovely lady—on the outside, at least. Unfortunately the inner woman remained a mystery.

Was Allison the world-weary snob she appeared to be? he mused. Or was she the vulnerable young woman who'd blinked back tears when Daisy hugged her? Meade simply didn't know. Would she let him get close enough to find out? he wondered.

Did he even want to?

Lost in visions of such an undertaking, Meade tossed the mail onto the buffet, snorting with impatience when it skidded right across the highly polished surface to land with a plop on the carpet. Meade gathered it up again, absently registering the usual junk and what could only be a bill from the local lumberyard.

Further investigation revealed that this bill was not the only one. Daisy had received what looked to be two others—from a veterinarian and from a dentist. Whirling, he strode into the kitchen just as Daisy stepped back inside from depositing her newest adoptees in their pen.

"Did you apologize to Allison like I told you to?" she immediately asked.

"Yeah, yeah," he answered, rather impatiently. He held out the mail. "These look like bills."

"They *are* bills," she replied calmly, taking them from him. "For the doghouse and pen, the cats' yearly shots and my root canal week before last."

"How on earth are you going to pay them? Unless you've had a sudden windfall, your budget is stretched to the limit."

"I'll pay *on* them," Daisy replied with a shrug, loading the dishwasher Meade had bought for her and which he knew she used only when he visited.

"But how?" he demanded in frustration. Not for the first time that day, he felt concerned about his aunt. "By starving yourself to death? Why didn't you tell me you needed some money? I would've sent it."

Daisy looked up and smiled, reaching to pat his cheek lovingly. "You've done enough for me already, Meade. Why, I'd be out on the street today if you hadn't bought this house from me when your Great-uncle Carl went into the nursing home. I can't let you do another thing."

"But you've always earned your keep and more," Meade pointed out, as usual calmed by her soft-spoken replies. "You find renters, keep the place going...." He sighed and shook his head. "Why won't you let me pay you a manager's salary like I used to? We had a good setup. I never worried about you going without."

"You paid me way too much," she told him with a decisive nod. "And I don't go without. Since you insist on paying all of the utilities, my only expenses are the phone bill, groceries and a few other sundries. With Carl's government check coming to me now, I can more than cover those."

"That check is for three hundred dollars, right?" Meade asked. At Daisy's nod of agreement, he mentally calculated what he knew of her budget from helping out with her income-tax return the past several years. Any way he figured it, she lived at poverty level—a fact he simply could not tolerate. "How can you feed all those cats, pay your bills and have any money left to spend on yourself?"

"I manage just fine," she replied, but Meade noticed she wouldn't meet his steady gaze. "Now stop worrying and tell me what you think of Allison."

Successfully sidetracked, Meade sat in silence before replying. He solemnly pondered Daisy's question, an echo of his own mere moments before, and he realized he still wasn't sure what he thought of Allison, other than the fact that he wanted her in his bed, of course.

In his bed? *Allison?* Meade almost choked at that errant thought.

They'd just met, for Pete's sake, and though that shocker of a kiss they'd shared told him there might be a woman of passion hiding under her supercool exterior, he seriously doubted he was up to the challenge of revealing her. She didn't seem to enjoy his company much. In fact, she didn't seem to enjoy *anyone's* company much. Meade couldn't help but wonder why.

"I think I'm going to have to spend some more time with her before I make up my mind," he hedged to Daisy. "She seems a little cool to me. Downright unfriendly, in fact. Any idea why?"

Daisy, now finished loading the dishwasher, herded Meade out of the kitchen toward the den. "I do have a theory," she admitted as they settled themselves in front of the television—Meade in the recliner, Daisy in her favorite rocker, cats everywhere. "I believe Allison has been hurt sometime in the past and is just making sure it won't happen again."

"What makes you say a thing like that?" Meade demanded, feeling oddly protective of Allison even though he suspected Daisy's answer might be the result of an overactive, very romantic imagination.

"Well, for one thing, she never gets mail from Nashville, at least none that I've seen." Daisy paused, reaching down to scoop up her current needlework project from a nearby basket. Then she slipped on her bifocals. "And she goes to great lengths to keep to herself. Why, I can hardly get a good-morning out of her." Daisy shook her head and began to stitch. "Worse than that, she never goes out with anyone, male or female. That's unnatural for a lovely young woman her age. It's almost as though she's afraid of getting involved in any kind of relationship. I'm really worried about her."

Relieved the evidence was only circumstantial after all, Meade scoffed at Daisy's theory. "If Allison weren't such an ice princess, she might have a few more friends," he said. "You're wasting your time worrying, and I can promise you that she wouldn't appreciate it a bit if she knew.''

"Shame on you, Meade Thomas Duran," Daisy scolded, abandoning her task long enough to shake a finger at him. "Just because that dear girl is more cultured than those flashy women you prefer is certainly no reason to assume she's cold." She went back to her sewing. "I think she could be a very loving person, and I think you had the right idea a minute ago. You should make an effort to get to know her better before you pass judgment."

An effort that might be the death of us all, Meade silently added, nonetheless considering her advice.

Upstairs in her tiny bathroom, Allison waited for the tub to fill with water. She slipped out of her clothes and stuffed them into the laundry chute that connected the two bathrooms in the house to the laundry room in the basement. Then she stepped on the digital bath scales from habit, barely noting the readout, since her thoughts were on her evening with the ''odd couple'' downstairs.

Though stressful, it had been rather enjoyable, especially when Daisy opened her presents. Allison smiled slightly, remembering the look on her landlady's face when she saw the brooch.

"I guess I might as well admit I care for her," she told her fogged-over reflection in the mirror. "And, whether I like it or not, she cares about me." That admission echoed in Allison's head, bringing to mind long-buried memories of loving and living with her grandmother.

She smiled slightly, remembering how very nice it would be to have someone to talk to, spend time with. What harm could it possibly do to let Daisy into her life? she asked herself. And so what if that sweet old woman tried a little mothering? Allison was due some, and who knows, she might even be able to manage a little "daughtering" in return.

Suddenly she felt warm all over, a feeling she knew had nothing to do with the steam emanating from the bathtub. Allison turned off the water and eased into the scented water until she could rest the nape of her neck on the high rim. She closed her eyes, relaxing now that she'd finally made a decision about Daisy.

But what about Meade Duran? her brain screamed.

Allison's eyes flew open. She sat up abruptly, frowning. Clearly she would get no rest until she came to some decision about him, too. That quick kiss in the hall had been a real eye opener, and the sexual chemistry between them confounded her. Had she imagined her shocking reaction? she suddenly wondered.

"Maybe if we kissed again," she mused, hastily adding, "just to see if I imagined it, of course."

Allison lay back again, her thoughts on that kiss. She remembered the tickle of Meade's mustache against her lip, the all-man smell of him. Her heart began to thud, telling her she had not imagined the impact of that brief caress.

So she hadn't imagined it. So what?

So bad news, she realized. His striking good looks and heart of gold were a lethal combination that could make an otherwise sensible woman overlook his annoying tendency to bossiness. Wasn't she, a woman who had sworn off men, now tempted to lower the barriers she had erected through the years since her divorce and risk kissing him again? Heaven forbid.

But then again, why shouldn't she? They were both single, after all. Attracted to each other. Entitled to a little fun.

Fun? Ha! There Allison's fantasy died. She knew better. One disastrous relationship was more than enough to convince her she wasn't looking for romance, or even friendship, from the male of the species. And though the idea might be tempting at times, she was no fool. Any kind of relationship with Meade Duran was as good as doomed before it began. Not only were they opposites, he would soon be back in Atlanta.

She had finally learned to live without love. She would be wise to avoid the likes of him.

Back downstairs, Meade said his good-nights and headed to Daisy's bathroom and the hot shower he hoped would soothe his tensed muscles. After ridding himself of his slacks, which he draped over a hanger on the back of the door, and his socks, which he tossed down the laundry chute, he hooked a thumb in the waistband of his briefs.

Suddenly Meade froze, sure he could hear singing. He stood immobile, straining to locate the source, and then pushed in the still-swinging door of the chute. Immediately he recognized Allison's voice, coming from the upstairs bathroom.

He might as well have been in the same room with her; she sounded that close. He heard water splash, and grinned, envisioning Allison shedding her clothes and stepping into Daisy's antique tub with its high sides and clawed feet....

At once Meade's grin vanished. He swallowed hard, wishing he didn't have such a vivid imagination. He could almost see her, up to her neck in bubbles, washing that gorgeous body, softly singing a love song.

Meade flushed from head to toe in heated response. Ice princess? Allison? Fat chance. The mere thought of her sent his temperature soaring.

Damn.

Ruthlessly Meade reached into the shower and turned on the cold water full blast. Gritting his teeth, he stepped under the stinging spray. It didn't help. He still burned to share another kiss with Allison—a deeper one this time, so he could relish the flavor of her. He also longed to do more with Allison, which Daisy probably hadn't had in mind when she suggested he get to know the renter better. How strange. Allison with her snobby ways and heart of stone was not his type of woman.

And physically attracted or not, he would do well to avoid the likes of her.

Chapter Four

Allison woke early the next day, full of anticipation. She lazed in bed for several minutes, trying to remember why and then denying the reason when she thought of him. She headed downstairs shortly after she rose, Merlin at her heels. Now firmly determined to cultivate a friendship with Daisy, she decided to join her for breakfast. Merlin simply wanted a saucer of milk.

"Good morning," Allison said when she entered the kitchen at seven-thirty. Daisy looked up from her coupon clipping in astonishment, then grinned her delight.

"Why, good morning," she said. "You're up awfully early for a Sunday."

"I wanted to catch you in the kitchen," Allison told her. "I was hoping I could talk you into making some more of those buttermilk biscuits you made for me my first morning in Memphis." She smiled, shyly adding, "I'll help, of course, and I'll make an omelet for you. That's *my* specialty."

"Of course I'll bake some biscuits," Daisy assured her, immediately abandoning her newspaper and Guinevere, who lay stretched out in her lap.

Now that wasn't so very hard, Allison thought, rather pleased with the result of her effort. She moved to the refrigerator to get the milk, ham and eggs she would need for her part of the bargain. In minutes Merlin had his saucer of milk and the two women stood side by side at the counter, measuring and stirring.

As always, Daisy chattered nonstop, mostly about her cats. Allison, more interested in her nephew—and in spite of all resolutions to the contrary—decided a gentle nudge in the right direction might be in order.

"Meade mentioned that his mother is American," she commented casually. "Is she your niece?"

"Actually she was my husband's niece. Meade and I aren't really blood kin, though I'm closer to him than any of my own relatives."

"You met for the first time when he was ten?"

"That's right," Daisy told her. "Twenty-nine years ago. He was just a youngster when his father was killed and his mother moved back to the States. She'd been living in Australia ever since she married Meade's father. Anyway, Meade was much younger than his three brothers and very angry about a lot of things, not the least of which was the move. He was always into trouble—though nothing serious, you understand—and his mother, who had to work, had her hands full keeping him in line."

"Is that where you came in?"

"Yes. I kept an eye on him after school until she got home at six. Meade and I hit it off from the beginning. I'm not sure why."

"I expect it was the cookies," Allison offered with a laugh. "He said you always had a plate of them waiting."

Daisy smiled. "Did he tell you that? Well, I did—and do—love to feed that boy. He's always had such a healthy appetite. And I enjoyed his company, too. My husband, Carl, sold insurance and traveled a lot. Since we weren't able to have children, I was alone a lot of the time. That little house was sure lonely before Meade moved in next door."

"Little house? You mean you didn't live here?"

"Oh, no," Daisy said. "Carl and I didn't buy this house until right before he retired. We thought the rental income would take care of the mortgage payments." She sighed heavily. "Poor Carl. He had a stroke barely a year after we bought it and was in a nursing home until he died four years later. Never did get to do the remodeling we'd planned."

Allison shook her head in sympathy. "Meade said you got him interested in karate," she prompted, changing the subject in hopes of putting the sparkle back in Daisy's eyes.

"I sure did," the older woman replied. She opened the oven to insert the pan filled with the biscuits she'd just rolled and cut out. "I got the idea one Saturday while watching one of those awful Japanese films with the subtitles. I did some calling around. Talked with a local instructor who kindly explained about the sport and the discipline involved. After deciding that was just what Meade needed, I dared him to try it. The rest is history, of course." She smiled. "Just between you and me, I never dreamed he would do so well at it."

"He's done well?" Allison poured her omelet makings into a heated pan.

"Oh my, yes. He's won oodles of trophies through the years. I have several of them in the bookcase in my bedroom."

"Does he still compete?" Allison asked, skillfully manipulating the gently bubbling mixture.

"His students do. And maybe he will again, once he gets away from instructing." She smiled proudly at Allison. "I'm so thrilled he's decided to start his own business. Now if he'd just get married to some nice young woman and have some babies . . ."

"Any prospects?" Allison asked, immediately regretting her impulsive question. It wouldn't do to have Daisy think she wanted to apply for the position of "nice young woman."

"None that I know of," Daisy replied. Apparently she thought nothing of the question and went on to add, "Thank goodness that last girlfriend of his moved on. She was such an airhead."

Allison bit her lip to keep from laughing at the unexpectedly modern term. "An airhead?"

"Yes, indeed. Definitely more bosom than brains." Daisy leaned toward Allison, whispering, "And just between you and me, I'll bet *they* were full of air, too."

Allison did laugh then. "I take it you didn't like her much."

"I didn't like her a bit. Or the girlfriend before her." She frowned. "I just don't understand why Meade can't attract the right kind of female. He's such a handsome man and so loving. I wonder if those locker-room manners of his have anything to do with it."

Though Allison definitely had an opinion about *that*, she tactfully didn't share it. Instead, she turned the omelet out onto a platter, while Daisy slipped her hand into a protective mitt to draw the golden-brown biscuits from the oven. "I guess everything is ready now. Why don't I go wake Meade?"

"That won't be necessary," Meade said from the door.

Allison and Daisy both whirled to face him, then exchanged a guilty look. "How long have you been up?" Daisy asked.

"Since five, when those damn dogs woke me," he muttered, wishing he'd followed his nose to the kitchen a few minutes earlier. Absolutely the last thing he'd expected to see this morning was Allison and Daisy cooking together. It was evident they'd been exchanging confidences like long lost friends just when he thought he had Allison pegged as a snob. Why the sudden camaraderie? he wondered.

"Oh dear," Daisy murmured. "I hope they didn't bother the neighbors. Mr. Luther doesn't need anything else to complain about."

"Did I tell you he came over yesterday morning?" Allison asked. "Arthur was in the bluebird box again."

"Bad boy!" Daisy exclaimed, shaking a finger at the cat, now sitting on the counter eyeing the omelet. She shooed him off and then hurried to the back door. "You two set the table. I'm going to check on the puppies."

The second she disappeared from view, Meade turned on Allison.

"What's going on here?" he demanded, highly suspicious of this unexpected friendship between his aunt and a woman he considered incapable of love. He didn't want Daisy to get hurt, intentionally or unintentionally.

"What do you mean by that?" Allison retorted, visibly bristling.

"How many times have you and Daisy breakfasted together on a Sunday morning?" He was closer now, deliberately using his height to intimidate her.

"Once," she told him. She'd squared her shoulders and raised her chin in response to his aggressive body language, but Meade noted that she carefully avoided his probing gaze.

"So what's going on?" he repeated, now certain she must have an ulterior motive for this display of affection. Just what that motive could be, he hadn't a clue.

"Nothing." Allison shifted her gaze to meet his head-on. "I was especially hungry this morning and Daisy just happened to be in here...."

Her voice trailed to silence under his unrelenting stare. She glanced away again, nervously clearing her throat. Obviously she felt uncomfortable about something, and determined to find out what, Meade reached out to cup her chin in his fingers. He turned her face to the light, trying to read her motives.

But he couldn't. She wore no makeup this morning and, without it, looked all of eighteen years old and as innocent as an angel. In spite of himself, Meade relished the sight of the freckles sprinkled across her upturned nose, the healthy glow of her unadorned skin. She smelled of soap—a scent he'd never considered sexy until this moment. Meade looked deep into her wide eyes, searching for ruthlessness, for deceit, for any reason not to trust her. Instead he found sincerity and...something else, something that touched the soft heart he'd always denied.

He found vulnerability.

It seemed as though Daisy might be right about Allison. She'd undoubtedly been hurt by something or someone and was afraid to let it happen again, a fact that would explain her solitary existence. Shocked by this discovery, Meade realized he wanted nothing more than to take her in his arms, reassure her...and kiss away the pain.

As though sensing his desire, Allison tugged his hand away from her face and stepped away from him.

"Sorry about that inquisition," he muttered, embarrassed by his bullying tactics. "I guess when it comes to Daisy's welfare, I sometimes get a little carried away. I can see you're just trying to be kind to her, and I hope *you* see how pleased she is.''

Cheeks now stained an attractive pink, Allison shrugged away his apology and explanation. ''Actually, I think it's going to be *my* pleasure,'' she said.

Then she smiled.

Meade's heart turned a backflip in response. Having stood all any mortal man could stand, he suddenly gave in to temptation. He pulled her into his embrace, taking her lips with a hunger that shocked them both. Allison tensed for a millisecond, then slipped her arms around his waist, pressing her lips and body against his. Her boldness delighted Meade, and he grunted with satisfaction when she tilted her head to accommodate his nuzzling lips. Her soft sigh of pleasure shimmied right up his spine. Too soon, she tried to pull away.

''I can't . . . I mustn't . . .'' Allison stammered, her words lost when he tightened his embrace and reclaimed her lips. She didn't resist at all this time; instead she opened her mouth to his teasing tongue.

Gently he explored the sweet interior of her mouth, savoring the flavor that was so distinctly Allison and every bit as wonderful as he'd expected.

''Meade, honey? Will you help me with the door, please?''

Lost in a barrage of sensation, Meade barely registered Daisy's call.

''Meade, Daisy needs you,'' Allison whispered, wedging her hands between them, trying to push him away.

He raised his head and stared blankly at her, struggling to get his brain to function again. ''Who?''

''Daisy. Your aunt,'' she prompted softly.

''Daisy!'' Meade released Allison and leaped back, dead certain he wasn't ready to explain to his aunt what had just happened. When a quick glance revealed she was outside and out of sight, he sucked air into his lungs, vainly trying to cool his overheated body.

"Be right there," he called, his voice still husky with desire. His gaze swept Allison, noting her flushed cheeks and bright eyes. She looked every bit as flustered as he felt, and thoroughly kissed, to boot. Only a fool wouldn't notice.

Daisy was no fool.

"Damn," he whispered, whirling to stride to the door.

Allison came to life, too, and in a flurry of activity snatched plates from the cabinet and forks from the drawer. Hastily she set the table, completing her task just as Daisy and Meade stepped into the room from the back porch. Daisy held a puppy in each hand.

"I've decided I'm going to let Robin and Marian stay inside until they get used to their new home," the woman explained, heading to the corner of the kitchen reserved for her pets. She placed them on a folded quilt. "Shouldn't take more than a few weeks."

A few weeks?

Allison, who'd never owned a pet in her life and hadn't even gotten used to having Merlin constantly underfoot, eyed the four mischievous cats and two rambunctious pups with trepidation. From across the room, Meade's dark eyes caught and held hers. Clearly he shared her reservations.

The fluffy omelet and buttered biscuits were a big hit with Meade. Daisy then begged him to accompany her to early-morning church services, a development Allison mentally applauded. Past ready to escape those piercing brown eyes of his, she gladly volunteered cleanup duty as added inducement. Her ploy worked, and less than an hour later found her listening anxiously for the slam of the front door, a sound that would tell her she was finally alone. She sighed her relief when she heard it and plopped down in one of the kitchen chairs.

"Did you guys see that?" Allison wailed to Daisy's newest four-footed friends, who were watching her with curious bright eyes from their box in the corner. "Why, I kissed that man like we were lovers. I must be crazy!"

Though the puppies didn't comment, Allison knew she was right. Hadn't she vowed to stay clear of Meade Duran *just last night*, for heaven's sake? Of course she had, and she'd meant every word. Yet one kiss, one lousy kiss, was all it had taken to melt her resolve.

Lousy kiss? Didn't she just wish! Meade's kisses were more... Allison frowned, searching for an adjective to do them justice. Several came to mind, among them "momentous," "mind-boggling" and "magical." Never had she responded so wantonly to a near stranger. No first-date kisser Allison Kendall. Yet she had known Meade a grand total of twenty-four hours, never been out with the man on a date and already she'd kissed him *three times*. How humiliating.

And how... exciting.

Shaking her head in bewilderment, Allison bent over to scoop up Merlin, who slept peacefully at her feet. "This is all your fault," she scolded.

He yawned his guilty conscience and, snorting her disdain of the male of *every* species, Allison abandoned him so she could unload last night's dishes from the dishwasher and reload it with that morning's. She worked automatically, her thoughts haunted by vivid memories of Meade's mustache tickling her lips, his gorgeous body pressed to hers.

It won't happen again, she promised herself with decided halfheartedness. Then, not convinced, she repeated the vow aloud and with fervor, shaking a clean fork at Merlin to emphasize her point. "It won't happen again."

"What won't happen again?"

Allison whirled at the sound of Meade's voice from right behind her. "You have a nasty habit of sneaking up on people," she snapped, taking a giant step back, one hand on her hammering heart.

He grinned and looked down at his size-twelve joggers. "It's the shoes."

"Why aren't you at church?" she demanded.

"Daisy remembered that she'd promised to keep the nursery during services today," he replied with a shrug. "She caught a ride with one of her friends, so I decided to go running in the park. Want to come?"

"No thanks," she said, grateful he would soon be out of reach, after all. Dressed in shorts and a muscle shirt that revealed most of his magnificent body, the man was a walking, talking temptation. Experience had shown her that she couldn't resist him. "Bye."

He frowned at her dismissal. "Are you trying to get rid of me?"

"As a matter of fact…" Allison's voice faded. No longer trusting herself to be near him, she stepped back so that the dishwasher door lay between them, a tactic not lost on Meade, whose eyes began to twinkle.

"Why?" he asked with a cocky grin. "Scared about what happened between us a while ago?"

Allison caught her breath at the intuitive guess and blushed. "Nothing happened," she quickly responded, embarrassed that he seemed to want to discuss something she'd just as soon forget.

Meade's grin vanished immediately and he glared at her. "If I'm not mistaken, we just kissed. Twice."

"Yeah, well, it won't happen again," she said, nodding sharply to reinforce her claim.

"Why not?" he asked. His eyes narrowed. "Didn't you like it?"

"No, I didn't," she bravely lied.

Meade agilely sidestepped the barrier to catch her shoulders in an iron grip. Rooted to the floor, she had no choice but to stand immobile while he read her expression. "You're lying, Allison."

"No, I'm—" She caught herself just in time. She *was* lying, something she abhorred. "Oh, all right. I did enjoy it . . . a little."

"I knew it!" Then he frowned. "Only a little?"

"I'm afraid so."

Once again Meade studied her face. "I think you're still lying."

Allison was, of course, but this time she had no intention of admitting it. Quickly she shook her head in denial.

Meade moved his hands to the counter on either side of her, the twinkle in his eyes now an unmistakable gleam of determination. He lowered his head as though to test her claim, but abruptly abandoned that idea when Allison impulsively wielded the fork she still clutched.

"Don't you dare," she warned, waving it under his nose.

Meade leaped back, throwing his hands up in mock terror. "Hey, now, there's no need to get hostile. I just thought another kiss might—"

"Think again."

Meade sobered at her clipped command. Clearly bewildered by this development, he shook his head slowly from side to side. "But why? Is there something wrong with me?"

"It's not that there's anything *wrong* with you exactly," Allison told him, silently adding a heartfelt wish that something were. "You're just not my type."

"What is your type?"

"I prefer men who are . . . less vocal, less physical."

"So I get on your nerves, huh?"

"In a word, yes," she said, cleverly omitting the fact that other body parts had fallen under his spell.

Meade sighed and leaned against the counter inches from her. His expression was gloomy. "I affect a lot of people that way," he said, all the light now gone from his eyes. "Most of the time I couldn't care less what anyone thinks of me. Then sometimes, like now, I care a lot." Startled by the unexpectedly candid admission, Allison hadn't begun to consider its implications when he shook his head and continued. "I just hope L. D. Crowley is more impressed with me than you are."

"L. D. Crowley?"

"An old friend I haven't seen in years and hope will give me financial backing for my project. We're meeting Saturday night to discuss it. Do you think there's any chance I can pull this off?"

Suddenly unwilling to hurt his feelings with an honest reply, Allison avoided answering and went to work on the dishwasher again. "Tell me more about this project of yours."

"I plan to start with just one center. We'll see how it goes and then, hopefully, build another, and then another. Who knows? Someday I might have one in every state."

She placed a stack of clean plates in the cabinet and then faced him. "I hate to burst your bubble, but aren't there already an awful lot of fitness centers around?"

"I'm not building a *fitness* center. I'm building a *wellness* center." When Allison frowned, Meade went on to explain, "I believe there's more to being fit than just working out on a machine or jogging a couple of nights a week. I believe in a total wellness program that includes not only physical fitness but mental fitness, too. I believe in prevention as opposed to cure and I think this is accomplished through education."

Allison saw that the glow was back in his eyes, but it was a different kind of glow this time, full of enthusiasm and optimism. Since she'd experienced exactly those emotions upon opening Etiquette, Etc., she understood them and smiled. "Tell me more."

"Well, in addition to the usual exercise programs you find in any fitness center in the city, I plan to offer classes on such health issues as nutrition and weight loss, high blood pressure and smoking cessation."

"Very interesting, but are you really qualified to do all that?"

"I'm hiring a dietitian and a therapist for the classes. I'll handle the physical fitness end of things myself."

"And these services will be targeted to families?"

"That's right, for all ages from infants to grandparents. Then eventually I hope to expand my focus. Maybe act as a consultant to large companies who wish to keep their employees fit and on the job. The possibilities for expansion are really endless."

"Sounds like a wonderful idea," Allison said, impressed by his business acumen. Clearly the muscle between his ears was as well developed as the rest of them. "I'll bet you'll do just fine."

"If I can find someone with enough vision to loan me the money," he grumbled, his frown back in place. "All the banks I've tried have given me a big, fat 'no.' If L.D. doesn't bite, I may never get this venture off the ground. Then there's the little matter of keeping it airborne once I do. Frankly, I don't know if I have what it takes to deal with the public. I'm always honest with people and sometimes a little impatient when they're not as goal-oriented as I think they should be.''

Allison, who could well believe that, understood his doubts. "All you have to do is think twice before you speak. Practice a little tact now and then.''

"Oh, yeah?"

"Sure. It's simple, really.''

"For you, maybe,'' he retorted. "Daisy tells me I don't have a tactful bone in my—'' Suddenly he broke off, slapping his flattened palm to his forehead. "Why am I worrying? You can teach me everything I need to know about getting along with people. We'll start tomorrow. Surely I'll be ready by Friday.''

Allison gaped at him, speechless with shock. Did he actually expect her to drop everything on her calendar and devote her days to him? Unbelievable! Why, even if she had openings next week she would never agree to such a scheme. It would be a total waste of her time. The man was way past saving.

Or was he? Hadn't she taken on worse in her career and succeeded? Of course she had. So what's the problem? Allison asked herself, at once suspecting it was more than anger at his presumptuousness. A brief examination of her topsy-turvy feelings revealed that her unexpected physical attraction to Meade was probably one of the sources of her negative feelings about helping out. What if she took him on and their relationship became more than a business association—as it could easily do if those fiery kisses were anything to go by?

"What time do you open for business in the morning?'' he asked, breaking into her thoughts.

"Nine, but there's no point in you showing up," she stated flatly before busying herself with reloading the dishwasher she'd finally emptied. "I'm booked solid for the next month. Why don't you ask Daisy to help you?"

"Because you're the expert. Surely you can find time for me."

"No, I can't, and even if I could, I wouldn't."

"And why is that?"

"Just because."

"That's a hell of an answer."

"Maybe so, but it's the only one you're going to get." Allison said the words with a bluntness born of sheer panic. As always, Meade's proximity had set her pulse to racing, reinforcing her belief that she should not become involved on any level with this man.

Red-faced and obviously frustrated, Meade opened his mouth as though to argue, but snapped it shut again. Then, without another word or a backward glance, he strode out the door, slamming it behind him.

Thankful he hadn't tossed out one of those irresistible "pleases" this time, Allison sagged weakly against the counter. She'd done it. She'd actually done it—resisted Meade Duran *and* made him angry, thereby ensuring that her days would return to their safe, uneventful sameness. She would probably see him only in passing from now on, and not even then if she were careful. In two weeks, he would be out of her life for good.

Chapter Five

Allison finished up her kitchen chores and headed upstairs about ten minutes later, with Merlin at her heels. As she entered her apartment, she took note of the silence that she usually relished but today found oppressive. It was almost as though the walls of her ivory tower were closing in on her.

Impatiently shaking off her uncharacteristic gloom, Allison settled herself on the love seat and picked up the remote control of her new TV. With a push of a button, she turned it on. She scanned each channel, looking for something to amuse her. She found nothing.

Feeling oddly bored and maybe just a little lonely, Allison abandoned the TV. She snatched up the old romance novel she had started rereading a couple of nights ago, and opened the dog-eared book to where she'd left off. While one part of her mind absorbed the plot, another part slipped down the street to jog alongside Meade. She could almost hear the sounds of a leisurely Sunday in the park, could feel the heat of the morning sun. She could also see just how he would look in action, muscles tensing with every long stride, sweat glistening on that gorgeous body....

Huffing her disgust with the graphic fantasy, Allison dragged her attention back to the novel. Get him out of your mind, she told herself, making a concentrated effort to focus on the printed words.

The golden firelight danced over the planes of his broad, bare chest as he stepped out of the shadows. Eyes blazing with desire, he reached out for her....

Allison slammed the book shut and flung it away. So much for relaxing. She leaped to her feet and began to pace the room in agitation, as usual talking to herself.

"I should have known this would happen. I should have known!"

Loneliness was nothing new to Allison, who'd learned the hard way to rely on herself for her happiness. She well understood how addicting companionship could be. Experience had shown her that she would suffer withdrawal every time she was alone again.

Why had she tangled her life with those of Meade and Daisy? she agonized, immediately wondering if it was too late to retreat. Maybe if she kept to her room, the two of them would get the hint and leave her alone. Then, when Meade was safely back in Georgia again, she could renew her friendship with Daisy, always taking care not to become too dependent on it, of course.

Surely it wasn't too late to do that. Surely.

Allison did manage to keep her distance the rest of Sunday, but at considerable expense. By the time she went to bed that night, she was actually willing to let Merlin curl up beside her—a first.

Monday morning she woke up late, the perfect reason to avoid breakfast and an early chat with her landlady. Gladly she made her excuses to Daisy and dashed out the door. Walking fast, she headed for Etiquette, Etc., situated in a shopping center about six blocks from Daisy's house.

By seven-thirty that night, the spring in Allison's step had definitely sprung. Exhausted after an interminable day with three rambunctious first-graders and a Miss Ideal Teenager-hopeful, Allison barely managed to drag herself home. She wanted only to bathe, settle herself on the love seat and, if she got a second wind sometime before midnight, heat up a can of soup or something for dinner.

With flagging spirits, Allison turned onto her own familiar sidewalk. She climbed the steps, groaning her weariness, and reached the porch just as the front door opened. Meade and Daisy stepped out, arm in arm and all smiles. Meade, no doubt still angry, acknowledged her presence with a stiff nod. Daisy wasn't so reticent.

"Why, hello, honey," she said with a smile, halting. "How was your day?"

"Hectic," Allison admitted, somehow mustering a smile of her own.

"Poor thing. I made a tuna casserole for lunch. Why don't you heat yourself up some of that?"

"Why, thanks," Allison murmured, touched by the gesture. "Are you two going out?"

"We certainly are," Daisy replied. "Meade's taking me to the Old Mill for dinner."

The Old Mill? Allison arched an eyebrow in surprise at the mention of the posh restaurant. Meade seemed more the pizza type to her. She couldn't help wonder how Daisy had talked him into a meal at such an elegant establishment, not to mention his wearing a suit and tie.

"We're having a dress rehearsal," Daisy explained, no doubt noting Allison's astonishment. "For his Saturday night meeting there with L.D."

"I see," Allison murmured, her gaze sweeping Meade. He looked extremely disgruntled with the whole thing and decidedly ill at ease.

"Then we're going for a spin in his car," Daisy added with a giggle, giddy as a teenager. "To the lake."

Allison listened silently to the rest of Daisy's plans, her climbing spirits taking another nosedive. What a treat it would be to go out to a really nice restaurant, she thought, almost wishing she had agreed to the etiquette lessons. She closed her eyes for just a moment, imagining herself dining with Meade and then taking a ride in that marvelous car of his. She could almost feel the night breeze on her face, smell the springtime flowers....

"Are you all right?" Meade demanded, grasping her arm.

"Just tired," Allison told him, now wide-eyed. She jerked free and, embarrassed to be caught daydreaming, moved determinedly toward the door.

Meade frowned and peered through the growing dark to the sidewalk. "Do you always walk to and from your office?"

"Yes," she replied. "That's just about the only exercise I get these days and the very reason I took this particular apartment."

"How often do you work this late?"

She shrugged. "A couple of nights a week, I guess."

"Is the street well lighted?"

Allison sighed her impatience with the sudden third degree. Two seconds ago he didn't care enough about her to mutter a hello. Now he was sticking his nose where it didn't belong—again. "You can see that it is."

"And what about your office? Is it secure? Do you feel safe?"

"Yes, yes," Allison told him. With a hasty goodbye, she waved them on their way and escaped inside. In the foyer, she paused to catch her breath and check the mail lying on the table. Absently she reached down to pet Merlin, who'd run up to greet her. He purred a welcome, then sashayed to the kitchen for his nighttime saucer of milk.

But Allison didn't follow tonight. Lost in a replay of the scene on the porch mere seconds before, she flipped through her mail, not really seeing any of it. She simply couldn't get over Meade's unexpected interest in her safety. No one but her grandmother had ever shown such concern for her welfare. And as annoying as it was, she felt rather flattered.

From the kitchen door, Merlin suddenly yowled his displeasure, a teeth-jarring sound that brought Allison abruptly back to reality. With a sigh of resignation, she reversed the order of her priorities for the evening and headed that way. Moments later found Merlin enjoying his milk and Allison rummaging around Daisy's side of the refrigerator for the casserole. She found it easily enough and closed the door, only to do a double take and yank it open again.

Her jaw dropped. Never in her life had she seen so much food jam-packed into one refrigerator. In fact, Daisy seldom bought more than a couple of sacks a week. Allison, never really giving the matter much thought, had attributed this to her landlady's dainty appetite or maybe the fact that she relied on a rather crowded senior citizens' bus for transport to the market. Money certainly didn't have anything to do with it. Daisy had to be well-off financially. She did own the house, after all, and Allison knew she received a government check in addition to her rental income. Maybe Daisy was simply taking advantage of Meade's vehicle and the opportunity to stock up. Or was she just trying to keep him fed?

Allison smiled at that and dished out a healthy portion of the casserole, which she heated in the microwave oven. Seconds later found her eating at the kitchen table, as alone as anyone could be with two dogs and five cats.

Five cats? Allison frowned and made a mental recount, bursting into laughter when she came up with the same total. The newest addition, a fluffy white Persian, lay stretched out on the windowsill, batting a paw at an ivy plant.

"Good for you, Daisy!" Allison exclaimed, pleased that her silver-haired landlady hadn't let Meade's opinion of her pets cramp her style. His loving concern for his aunt often bordered on interference, to Allison's way of thinking, and given half the chance he would gladly run Daisy's—and, it seemed, Allison's—lives. Not that it wasn't nice to be the object of such attention every now and then. But there were limits, and Meade seemed the sort of man who might ignore them.

"Is something wrong, dear?" Daisy asked Meade, barely an hour later.

He jumped guiltily. "What?"

"Is something wrong?" Daisy repeated. "You haven't eaten a bite of your steak."

He glanced at the huge piece of meat on his plate and dutifully picked up his fork and knife. "I can't swallow," he complained. "This damn tie is choking me to death."

"It's not the tie, it's the shirt," she countered. The flickering lanterns hanging on the roughly hewn walls put a decided twinkle in her gray eyes. "Why don't you buy one that's big enough in the neck?"

"Because they don't make them!" Meade snapped, immediately regretting his tone of voice. "Hell, Daisy. I'm sorry. It isn't your fault I suddenly feel like I was raised in a barn."

"It isn't your mother's, either. You should have listened to that poor woman when she was trying to teach you and those heathen brothers of yours how to behave in public."

"No. I should've picked the meeting place instead of letting L.D."

"Well, what's done is done," Daisy replied, taking a minuscule bite of her filet mignon. She chewed in thoughtful silence for a moment before adding, "And you're going to have to make the best of the situation. Frankly I don't understand why you're so worried. You and L.D. got along marvelously when you lived next door to each other."

"That was twenty-five years ago, for Pete's sake, and I never asked for money. Why, L.D.'s taken a simple accounting firm and turned it into a multimillion-dollar financial institution. What possible reason could someone like that have for backing a loudmouthed karate instructor with big ideas but little experience?"

"Don't be so hard on yourself. The fact that you prefer hot-dog stands to restaurants has nothing whatsoever to do with your ability to run a wellness center. You've been the athletic director of one of the state's more influential private schools for going on ten years. L.D. would be an idiot not to recognize the value of that."

Meade sighed and abandoned the perfectly grilled steak. "I guess it's more than just the dinner on Saturday, Daisy. I keep thinking about getting that loan and then falling flat on my face. I've been working with teenagers who had no choice but to stick with the program whether they liked me or not. It won't be like that once I open the center, and I don't know if I've got what it takes to get along with adults." He shook his head. "I just wish Allison would've agreed to help me out. Those lessons would've made a difference. I'm sure of it."

"What exactly did you say to her?"

"I asked if she would be willing to teach me a few social skills this week and she—"

"You asked?"

"Yes, and she—"

"Asked?"

Meade glared at Daisy. "That's right."

"Did you really *ask* her?" she questioned, glaring right back. "Or did you *tell* her."

Meade opened his mouth to reply, then shut it, his conversation with Allison coming back loud and clear. "I, uh, guess I told her."

"Then it's no wonder she turned you down," Daisy scolded. "Some of us don't like to be told what to do."

Meade avoided her accusing gaze by letting his own sweep the dimly lit room. He noted the split-log floor, caneback chairs and rock fireplace so often found in restaurants these days. What made this particular establishment so special? he suddenly wondered. Frowning slightly, he shifted his gaze to the linen tablecloths, the crystal goblets, the mirrored ceilings. Suddenly he saw the answer: contrast.

The dining room was neither too elegant, nor too rustic. It was a blend of both worlds—exactly what he needed to be. But how could he accomplish such a feat without help?

"Maybe if you approached Allison again," Daisy said, as though reading his thoughts. "Maybe if you asked very sweetly—"

"You mean beg?" he interjected, horrified.

"I was thinking more along the lines of a bribe." Daisy glanced to each side, as though checking for eavesdroppers. Then she leaned toward Meade, motioning for him to move closer. She lowered her voice. "I have an idea...."

Yawning, Allison sat on the side of the bed and reached automatically for her alarm clock. After noting the time—ten-fifteen—she set it to buzz at six the next morning and then crawled between the crisp pastel sheets, snuggling into her fluffy feather pillows. A soft plop seconds later signaled the arrival of Merlin, who nosed his way under the covers to curl up beside her. Allison toyed with the idea of shooing him away, but murmured, "Only for a minute" instead.

The minute stretched into five and then ten. His melodic purr hypnotized her, and Allison relaxed in stages until she finally fell asleep. Hours—or was it seconds?—later, she sat bolt upright in bed, jerked back to wide-eyed consciousness by a knock on the door and a very familiar male voice urgently calling, "Allison, it's Meade. I have to see you."

At midnight? Thinking something must surely have happened to Daisy, Allison sprang from bed, grabbing a terry robe and pulling it on as she charged through the living room.

"What is it?" she demanded breathlessly when she opened the door. "What's wrong?"

"Nothing's wrong," he quickly assured her. "I'm sorry if I woke you. I had no idea you'd be in bed so early."

"Early?" Allison glanced at her watch, noting it was only ten forty-five. She drew in a deep breath to soothe her shattered nerves and then wrapped the robe more tightly around her. "What do you want, Meade?"

"I really need to talk to you. May I come in, please?"

Allison eyed him warily, certain he was up to no good. "I'm not dressed for male callers."

"You look fine to me," he responded, to her surprise adding, "But if you prefer, I can come back tomorrow."

Choices? From Meade Duran? Thrown off guard, Allison found herself muttering, "I guess it would be all right, if you don't stay long."

"Thanks." He stood immobile until she stepped back to let him enter and then went no farther into the apartment than the edge of the door. Downright uneasy at this uncharacteristic display of good manners from a man who'd been known to barge his way in, Allison nonetheless led him to the love seat. Meade took a seat on one end of it, murmuring his thanks.

Her eyes never leaving his face, she perched lightly on the edge of the nearby rocker. Clearly Meade Duran wasn't himself tonight, and Allison didn't quite know what to make of it.

"Daisy and I discussed your situation over dinner," he told her. "We've come up with the perfect solution to your problem."

"What situation? What problem?" she blurted, baffled.

"You're single."

Allison frowned. "That's a problem?"

"It can be if you're also stubborn."

He had her attention now, and though somewhat miffed at being called stubborn, she was just curious enough to ignore the insult. "All right, I'm hooked. What *are* you talking about?"

"Your safety. Are you aware that there have been a couple of robberies on this side of town in the past month?"

"I did know that, yes."

"And are you aware that one of Daisy's best friends, Erma Something-or-other, was mugged in the park this afternoon?"

Allison caught her breath in shock. "*Our* park?"

He nodded solemnly, repeating, "This afternoon."

She swallowed hard. "Was she hurt?"

"Just shaken up, but her purse was stolen."

"Poor thing."

Meade got to his feet and began to prowl the room restlessly, his brows knitted together in a worried frown. The silence grew deafening before he halted by her chair and dropped to one knee beside her, crossing his arms over the armrest. "Daisy is worried about you. She thinks you should stop working so late."

"But I can't," Allison argued, swaying back slightly so she'd have access to air *not* laced with the scent of his spicy after-shave. "Why, at least a fourth of my clients have to come in after hours."

"Then drive your car instead of walking."

She shook her head. "I can't do that, either."

"Can't, or won't?" Meade asked softly, reaching out to gently tug a lock of her hair.

That unexpectedly playful action in the middle of such a serious conversation disconcerted Allison, who was suddenly intensely aware of his nearness. She slapped his hand away and got to her feet, putting precious distance between them. "Won't, and why should I? I have every right to walk the streets—day or night—and no mugger is going to take that right away." She squared her shoulders and glared at Meade, fully expecting him to rage his disagreement.

Instead he got to his feet, too, calmly nodding. "I agree and that's what I told Daisy. She wasn't convinced, unfortunately."

"Well, I'm really sorry she's worried about me, but there's nothing I can do to ease her mind."

"Oh, but there is," Meade said. "And that's why I'm here tonight. I'd like the opportunity to check out security in your office. I'm no expert, of course, but I have given workshops with the police department on self-defense and security for the past five years and learned a lot of valuable hints I'm more than willing to pass along to you. I'll even throw in a few self-defense techniques—simple ones that just might give you an edge if you were ever attacked. That should satisfy Daisy."

"I see," Allison murmured, crossing her arms over her chest and eyeing him with suspicion. "And just what would you expect in return for all your labors?"

Meade grinned. "I think a few lessons in the social graces might be a fair exchange."

"That's just what I figured." She walked to the door and stood there, toe tapping her irritation at his attempt to manipulate her. "Sorry, Meade. Not interested."

To her astonishment, he merely shrugged. "I told Daisy you wouldn't go for it, but she seemed to think you would."

"She did?"

"Yeah. She said a levelheaded young woman like you would jump at the chance to ensure your independence."

"And what did *you* say?"

"I said you had too much pride to admit you just might need me as much as I need you."

Allison tilted her head back, returning his steady gaze in thoughtful silence. So he thought her proud, huh? Well, he was right. She *was* proud, but not too proud to admit that his idea just might have merit. What possible harm could it do to have Meade check out the security of that old building that housed her office? she wondered. And while he was there, why couldn't she could give him just enough etiquette lessons to boost his esteem?

As for the self-defense nonsense, well, she simply couldn't imagine herself downing an assailant with a shout and a chop. Besides, that sort of lesson would, no doubt, involve physical contact, something Allison intended to avoid at all costs.

"This alliance would be strictly business?" she questioned sharply, at once remembering their last devastating physical contact. "No more stolen kisses?"

"Not unless you're the bandit," he replied.

Still she hesitated. "I'd have to work you into my schedule since I already have a full week, and I'm closing shop early on Friday to help Daisy get ready for her dinner."

He grinned. "No problem. I'm at your disposal, day or night."

Oh, Lord. "All right, then. We'll start tomorrow around five-thirty."

"Hot damn!" Meade exploded, catching Allison in a bear hug that lifted her right off the ground. He kissed her soundly, then set her back on her feet, cutting off her immediate protest with a solemn, "Last time, I swear," before striding out the door and down the steps.

Senses reeling, lips atingle, Allison stared after him. "Oh, my God," she muttered. "What have I done?"

Chapter Six

Tuesday evening at five-forty Allison sat alone in her office, waiting for Meade to arrive. She chewed the eraser of her pencil, staring out the window instead of at the accounts that needed balancing. Then she looked at her watch again, wondering if he might have changed his mind about the lessons. While the pragmatic side of her hoped he had, another side—the secret, highly romantic side that had taken special pains dressing that morning—hoped he was just running a little late.

Tossing down her pencil, Allison rose abruptly and walked into the tiny bathroom off her office. A quick peek in the full-length mirror revealed a passably attractive businesswoman dressed for the part in a tasteful linen suit. She fumbled nervously with her silk scarf, draping it first one way and then another before throwing her hands up in exasperation and huffing her impatience with her uncharacteristic nervousness.

What's the matter with me? she wondered. I'm not trying to knock his socks off. I just want to impress him with my professionalism.

Sure you do, the romantic in her taunted. Allison sighed and picked up a hairbrush, her thoughts on the lonely years since her divorce from Charles Wren, a broker she married right out of college. Feeling a little at loose ends after the hectic days of campus life and desperate for a "family" she could call her own, Allison had married in haste. She'd given her all to her husband, a taker who accepted everything, never giving anything in return. He made it quite clear that his clients and their investments would always come before quiet nights in each other's arms.

Allison, who'd been virtually deserted as a toddler by career-minded parents, believed she had paid her dues to the business world and deserved better than a halfway relationship this time. She did her best to save the misbegotten union, finally giving up on her big dreams of a loving, attentive husband and a houseful of children only when certain there was no chance for them. Clearly she was meant to live her life alone. That was why her career meant everything to her these days. That was why she knew better than to let these lessons with Meade be anything other than strictly business.

Something in her sensed he could easily tear down the barriers she had so carefully erected to protect her heart. She had no intentions of letting that happen or of opening herself up to disappointment again. Especially not with a domineering man like Meade, who would never appreciate the independent woman she had finally become.

That reaffirmed, Allison spent the next several minutes vigorously brushing out her long hair and then twisting it to form a stern knot at the nape of her neck.

"Allison? Where are you?"

She started at the sound of Meade's voice from the reception area of the office suite. Abandoning her attempts at a new hairdo, she quickly shook her hair out and exited the bathroom.

"I was beginning to think you'd changed your mind," Allison greeted Meade with professional coolness. Her eyes took a not-so-professional note of his khaki pants, which hugged muscled thighs, and the light sprinkling of curly dark hair revealed by the V neck of his ivory cotton sweater. Her heart turned a somersault in a purely feminine response that demolished her composure, not to mention her big plans to keep things strictly business.

"Naw," he replied, standing by the counter that separated the waiting area from the desk a receptionist would someday occupy. "I couldn't find a parking place."

"Another reason I walk to work," she commented with a calmness she did not feel. "The lot is always full during the day—spillover from the condos next door, I suspect. I hate to take up unnecessary space."

He nodded and glanced around the room. "Very nice. I like it."

"Thanks," Allison said, unable to hold back her smile of pride. The office *was* nice and worth every personal sacrifice she made so she could pay the rent. "Would you like the grand tour?"

"Sure."

Highly aware of him and therefore anxious to get this evening over with, Allison slipped into the waiting area. She then led the way down a short hall.

"In addition to the reception area and my office," she told him as they walked, "I have a small lounge and this classroom." She stepped into the room, which was furnished with a podium, student desks, blackboard, television and videocassette player. "I thought it might be best if we worked in here. Do you have any objections?"

"Not a one," Meade said. "But we may have to scoot some of the desks out of the way when I demonstrate my self-defense techniques."

"About that..." Allison cleared her throat and prepared to do battle if that was what it took to talk him out of those lessons. She dared not risk getting that close to him, not when they were so very alone and she had an acknowledged susceptibility. "I really don't see any point in wasting your time or mine on this self-defense mumbo jumbo. I'm just not into that sort of thing and I'd never use it anyway."

"Whatever you say," Meade agreed, seating himself at one of the desks, which proved to be rather inadequate for a man of his stature. He shook his head doubtfully. "Maybe we'd better get started on the etiquette lessons right away. I'm not sure how long I'm going to be able to sit here."

Once again disconcerted by his size—not to mention his easy acceptance of a decision she'd dreaded to share—Allison took a moment to reply. "Why don't we begin with everyday manners? I have several handouts prepared. We'll look at that one together." Seating herself a safe distance away from his considerable male charm, Allison carefully reviewed the material, which turned out to be a common-sense approach to behavior based upon kindness and consideration.

The comprehensive handout was quite an eye opener to Meade, who had no idea there was so much more than "ladies first" to learn. Barely an hour after they started the lesson, he decided he'd had enough for this sitting.

"It's nearly seven," he interjected when Allison finished that handout and reached for another. "Why don't we call it 'lesson one'? I'd like to point out the security problems I spotted when you were showing me around the place.''

"You really saw problems?" She seemed dubious. That didn't surprise Meade, who ran into doubters every time he helped with a self-defense and safety workshop.

"Several," he told her with a let's-get-to-business nod. He got to his feet and stretched, trying to ease his cramped muscles. Then he walked over to one of the windows to tap on it. "Let's begin with these. I suggest a change to metal frames with small panes of shatterproof glass."

"That makes sense, I suppose," Allison agreed from where she still sat.

"I'd also suggest rearranging the room so that this podium—" he grasped the edge of the solid wooden structure "—is at the other end, by the exit."

"Now *that* I don't understand," she commented, getting slowly to her feet to join him. "What difference does it make where I stand when I teach?"

"A lot, if one of your clients suddenly gets amorous."

Allison laughed heartily at that. "Don't be absurd."

"Listen," Meade responded, glaring at her. "You're a beautiful young woman. It's not inconceivable that one of your male clients might be tempted to go beyond the student-teacher relationship."

Beautiful young woman? The unexpected compliment caught Allison off guard, flustering her.

"Have you thought about what you'd do if one of them suddenly made a grab for you?" Meade asked.

"Of course I haven't. But you can rest assured that if the occasion arose—and I'm certain it never will—I *could* take care of myself."

"Prove it," he said. "You be the teacher. I'll be the student. Show me what you'd do if I made a pass."

She panicked. "I really don't think that's a good idea."

"Humor me." His dark eyes pleaded with Allison, robbing her of her common sense until she could come up with no good reason to refuse.

"Oh, all right, but I feel like an idiot."

"No one's going to see us," Meade told her. "Now stand at the blackboard like you're writing something on it. I'll sit here."

He moved to one of the desks and sat down. Allison hesitated, then turned her back on him to pick up a piece of chalk. She heard the squeak of the desk and whirled just as Meade engulfed her in his powerful embrace, pinning her arms to her sides.

"Gotcha!" he said, his warm breath fanning her face. "Now what are you going to do about it?"

Disconcerted to find herself heart to heart with him after all her errant thoughts, Allison gulped, then wiggled to test the extent of her capture. Meade responded by tightening his hold, an action that crushed her breasts against the wall of his chest. Her blood boiled in response.

"You're going to have to do better than that," he teased softly.

Allison wasn't sure she could. Her knees were about to buckle, and her arms, which seemed to have a mind of their own, slipped around his waist. To her horror, she found herself returning the embrace instead of breaking out of it. Oh so gently she brushed her lips against the pulse in his neck.

He caught his breath. "Allison?"

"Hmm?" She nuzzled his Adam's apple.

"You're not trying to get away."

"No." Breathless and burning for him, Allison gave in to her need. She raised up on tiptoe, hungrily pressing her mouth to his. Meade groaned fiercely and responded with a savage intensity. He took control of the kiss, deepening it by teasing her teeth apart with his tongue. He trailed his lips to her earlobe, and with a soft moan, Allison tipped her head to one side, baring the sensitive flesh of her neck to his exploration. His beard, surprisingly soft, caressed her cheek and chin. Goose bumps danced down her arms.

Robbed of her strength, she clung to him, and eternity passed before he raised his head, pulled free and stepped back. He ran his fingers through his hair, laughing shakily. "Your technique is original. Ineffective as hell, but definitely original."

Abruptly Allison came to her senses. Her face flamed at the realization of what she had just done. "I—I don't know what to say," she stammered, mortified. "I don't usually attack my students."

"Maybe I should teach *them* self-defense."

Was that actually a twinkle she saw in his eye? Was that lilt in his voice laughter? Allison bristled, and her responding fury almost choked her. "This is not funny! I've never done anything so unprofessional in my whole life."

"Hey," he said, reaching out to clasp her arms and give her a little shake. "Lighten up. It was just a kiss, for Pete's sake."

Just a kiss? She wanted him so badly that she had actually lost control, and he called it "just a kiss." Damn.

Allison closed her eyes, counting to ten and then twenty while she struggled to regain her composure. Clearly he didn't realize the depth of her desire for him. Maybe if she played her cards right, he never would. She opened her eyes again, forcing an airy smile. "You're right, of course. It's perfectly normal for...*friends* to share a kiss every once in a while."

He grinned and nodded. "Sure it is. Even if one of them only enjoys it 'a little.'"

Allison blushed to her toenails at his deliberate reference to yesterday's lie. He hadn't believed her then and didn't believe her now. No wonder. She squirmed with embarrassment.

"Of course," he continued as though oblivious to her torment, "it would make even more sense if they both enjoyed it a lot."

Things were getting worse by the second. He was so calm, so cool, so...casual. Fiery kisses such as the one they'd just shared were no doubt an everyday occurrence for a man like him. Unfortunately they weren't for Allison, who hadn't kissed a man with that much abandon in years.

Years? Ha. Who was she trying to fool? She'd *never* kissed a man like that, not even good ol' Charlie.

Allison fumbled for something clever to say, something that might convince Meade that she, too, played these man-woman games all the time and knew the rules. But, as usual, honesty won out.

"Look, Meade. Since you've probably already guessed, I may as well admit I'm not as practiced at casual flirtations as you obviously are. I have no excuse for what just happened except to say that it's been a long day and I'm obviously not thinking clearly. I apologize, and I swear it won't happen again. Now could we please just call it a night and go home?"

"Sure," Meade responded as though she hadn't just bared her soul to him. "Right after I show you how to break free of that kind of hold." To her horror, he reached out, unexpectedly tugging her into his arms once more.

"What are you doing?" Allison screeched, her just-back-to-normal pulse rate going berserk again.

"Showing you how to escape," Meade replied. As if the kiss had never happened, he demonstrated the technique—a fist worked between their bodies and pressed firmly into the captor's diaphragm.

"It works!" she exclaimed minutes later when she'd successfully mastered the maneuver. All her embarrassment was momentarily forgotten in the excitement of her new knowledge. "And it's so simple. Come on, show me something else."

To her surprise, Meade shook his head. "Not tonight. I'm starved, and I promised Daisy I'd pick up a pizza on the way home. She's probably given me up by now." He walked to the exit. "Let's go. I'll show you the other security problems as we leave."

Allison followed him to the reception area.

"You need a bell on the door," he said. "Or some other noisemaker. It doesn't matter what, as long as you can tell when someone comes in." He reached out, grasping and turning the doorknob. "A better lock is definitely in order, too. I'd suggest a dead bolt, which can make a door virtually impenetrable. And it wouldn't hurt to invest in security strips while you're at it. They set off an alarm if anyone tampers with them."

"Thanks for the tips. I promise to talk to my landlord about tightening security. Now let's get out of here."

They did moments later and walked through the nearly deserted parking lot to his car. Meade pointed out the folly of parking anywhere but right outside her office on the days she drove. He cautioned her to stay well away from other cars and to walk with her head up and her eyes alert to possible danger.

Allison found herself edging closer to him as they entered a particularly shadowy section of the lot. Meade glanced down at her and, as though picking up on her unease, lay an arm across her shoulders.

He unlocked his car, and Allison slipped inside. Resting an arm on the top of the passenger door, he bent down to peer at her. Suddenly eye to eye with Meade, Allison forgot any nervousness, remembering instead how it felt to be mouth to mouth, body to body with him.

"I'm not really trying to scare you," he said, gently brushing her flushed cheek with his fingertips. "I just want you to use your head." With that he shut the door and headed for the driver's side.

Use your head. The advice echoed loudly in her brain, bringing vividly to mind the folly of her actions thus far that night. The kiss had meant nothing to Meade. It had meant everything to her. She was headed for a heartache if she didn't get a grip on reality and her roller-coaster emotions.

Duly chastised, she renewed her determination to keep their association strictly business. By the time Meade got in beside her, Allison had taken his advice, at least in matters of the heart.

Meade said little during the ride to the pizza parlor and then on to Daisy's. His thoughts were back in Allison's office, mentally replaying that incredible self-defense lesson he'd so cleverly managed to work in. Her kiss had been a shocker, catching him by surprise, throwing him off balance as effectively as any technique he could teach her.

He remembered Allison's obvious chagrin at her "unprofessional" actions. He'd felt the same at his own behavior, and he hoped he'd successfully hidden it from her. Never in his career as a martial-arts instructor had he responded sexually to one of his female students. Yet the moment he'd wrapped his arms around Allison tonight, his professionalism had disintegrated.

Intensely aware of the smell and feel of her, he'd foolishly responded to Allison's surprising kiss and given in to his need to taste her, too. He didn't know how he finally found the strength to break the kiss; he didn't know how he found wits to make light of the whole thing. He did know that if he'd been crazy enough to agree to another self-defense demonstration, they'd have wound up practicing holds no instruction manual boasted.

And Daisy would still be waiting for her pizza.

So what now? he asked himself. And what about tomorrow night? Allison expected another lesson exchange. Could he maintain his professionalism enough to handle it? And what if he couldn't?

It all depended on Allison, he realized. He was ready to take as much as she would give him, ready to give as much as she would take.

Or was he? Her kisses said she wanted Meade as badly as he wanted her. Yet she'd as good as said she wasn't into casual sex. Since he wasn't into that sort of relationship either at this point in his life, that left only a long-term affair that would continue even after he returned to Georgia.

As intriguing as Meade found that possibility, he knew the timing wasn't right. He had just committed himself to a career change. He had to devote his full energies to it. Besides, he and Allison were opposites, and any romantic alliance between them—short- or long-term—could only end in disaster, no matter how stimulating.

"Meade, turn!" Allison exclaimed, breaking into his reverie. He hit the brake and headed into Daisy's drive on two wheels, shrugging sheepishly when Allison grabbed the pizza box to keep it from flipping onto the floor.

"Sorry," he muttered.

She gave him a hard look, then reached for the door handle.

"Wait," he blurted. "I need to talk to you."

She waited.

"I believe I owe you an apology," he said, deliberately choosing words that would enable him to regain control of their situation. "I tricked you into that self-defense lesson tonight and I shouldn't have. Especially after you told me you weren't interested."

"It's okay." Again she reached for the door handle. Again he halted her.

"No, it isn't," he argued, smoothly adding, "And I'll understand if you want to break our bargain and cancel the rest of the lessons."

"But you have so much more to learn," she said. "And so do I."

Well, hell. "You mean you actually want to go on with this?"

"Definitely," she said. Then she frowned. "Don't you?"

"I, uh . . ." Meade hesitated, caught between his need to get out of the lessons and his fear she would guess the true state of his hormones.

Allison sighed. "You're afraid I might attack you again, aren't you? Well, I promised to behave, and I will. I really should take advantage of this opportunity. You're such a good instructor—surprisingly patient, extremely knowledgeable."

In big trouble, he silently added, with a hard swallow. He finally admitted to himself that where Allison was concerned, he might never have control of the situation. She was too unpredictable. "Then I guess we're still on."

"Thanks." One more time, she put her hand on the door. "Can we go in now? I'm this close—" she pinched her thumb and forefinger together "—to eating the pizza right here."

Meade nodded numbly, took the box from her and stepped out of the car. He slowly followed Allison up the walk and onto the porch, wondering with every step how she'd managed to throw him off balance yet again. Just as she opened the screen door, Daisy's newest adoptee dashed between his legs and into the house, very nearly tripping him.

"Damn cat!" he exploded, rudely reminded of another situation over which he apparently had no control. He readjusted his grip on the box to keep from dropping it.

Allison smiled. "I noticed our latest addition last night. Where'd he come from and what's his name?"

"He's a she—Morgan Le Fay—and Daisy rescued her from a German shepherd in the parking lot of the grocery store yesterday."

"Isn't that sweet?" Allison murmured, her eyes dancing with suppressed laughter.

"Sweet" wasn't at all the word Meade had in mind. But certain Allison wouldn't want to hear the one he'd thought of, he wisely held his peace. Her amusement told him she approved of Daisy's action and would probably feel compelled to defend the older woman again. While a good row might be the answer to his current problem—Allison surely wouldn't want to continue the lessons, then—it might strain his relationship with Daisy.

Meade couldn't chance that happening. He adored his aunt and owed her a tremendous debt for helping him through some very traumatic years. He intended to be around to see that she lived a happy, worry-free existence until the end of her days.

That wouldn't be easy, of course, since she refused to accept any financial aid from him. All he could do was stand helplessly on the sidelines, watching while she squandered her meager income on her pets. Not that he didn't like animals. He did. And if Daisy had to be up to her elbows in cats to be happy, he didn't give a damn. Hell, she could start her own zoo for all he cared, *if* she fed herself first and occasionally bought a new dress. But as long as she wouldn't take any money from him, the cats were a nuisance, to Meade's way of thinking. They took food from her mouth, clothes from her back.

Unfortunately Daisy would never agree with that, a fact that frustrated Meade to no end and was the reason he invariably blew his top whenever the subject came up, no matter how hard he tried not to.

"It's about time you two got home!" Daisy greeted them as they stepped into the hallway. "Did you remember to ask for extra mushrooms?"

Meade had to smile. "I did," he replied, handing her the box.

Daisy took it and led the way to the kitchen, flipping on the light as she entered the room. "I have no business eating this, not with the trouble I've been having with my stomach. But every once in a while I crave pizza." She set it on the table and opened the box, exclaiming her delight. "Meade, get the plates. Allison, get the iced tea. Let's eat."

Allison and Meade complied, and in a matter of minutes, the three of them were seated around the table, eagerly consuming the extralarge, superdeluxe delicacy.

"What did you learn tonight?" Daisy asked her nephew between bites.

He frowned. "Not nearly enough. I didn't know there were so many rules to remember. I'll never be ready for the world by Saturday."

"Maybe you should just concentrate on table manners so you can get through your dinner appointment," Daisy said. "Then next week, when you aren't so pushed for time, Al-

lison can give you some in-depth lessons that will help you
deal with the public.''

"No!"

Allison and Daisy both jumped at his vehement reply. He
flushed at their curious stares. "I, uh, don't want to take up
any more of her valuable time than necessary. She's a very
busy lady."

"Oh, I could probably work you in all right," Allison
said. "But it shouldn't be necessary if you'll just apply
yourself and review the handout I gave you between lessons."

"I'll start tonight," Meade hastily agreed, wondering
where the heck it was. He'd been so distracted by the self-
defense lesson, he'd forgotten all about it.

"And what did *you* learn?" Daisy asked Allison before
helping herself to another slice of pizza.

"I learned what to do if I'm suddenly caught up in a bear
hug by one of my students," the brunette replied. Her immediate wince and subsequent look of guilt told Meade she
just might wish she hadn't been quite so honest.

"What *do* you do?" Daisy asked her, wide-eyed with
interest.

Meade, who wanted to hear the answer to that one, too,
stared intently at Allison. She squirmed under his accusing
look, her cheeks staining an attractive pink. "You, uh,
punch him in the solar plexus. Knock the wind right out of
him."

Since that summed up exactly what had happened—and
before he showed her proper technique—Meade felt his
own face flushing. Steadfastly he avoided further eye contact with Allison, instead shifting his gaze to his plate and
the pizza that had suddenly lost its taste.

"Goodness," Daisy exclaimed, clearly intrigued. "And
what are you going to teach her tomorrow night?"

Meade tried to think up a harmless maneuver, one that didn't involve frontal contact. "How to get out of a rear headlock."

"My, my," Daisy said. "This is so exciting. I can hardly wait until Friday night to learn a few of these tricks myself. You never can tell when a date might get out of hand, you know."

Meade's jaw dropped. *A date?* Did Daisy have a boyfriend? He opened his mouth to ask her, shutting it again when someone knocked on the back door. "I'll get it."

He walked to the door and opened it to find a man and woman standing on the steps holding a bouquet of wilted chrysanthemums.

"Is Daisy here?" the man, who looked to be fiftyish, demanded.

"Why, Jacob Newman," exclaimed Daisy, joining Meade at the door. "And Reba. How nice of you two to drop in. Have you met my great-nephew, Meade Duran? He's here for a visit. Meade, this is the couple who live in that beautiful red brick house a couple of doors down, the one with all the flowers."

"We didn't come over to visit, Miss Daisy," Reba interjected, unsmiling. "We came to talk to you about your cat."

Daisy tensed visibly. "Oh? Which one?"

"The Persian. We chased it out of our yard several minutes ago," Jacob Newman said. "It ran right onto your porch about the time your nephew drove up."

"Why were you chasing her?" Daisy asked.

"She wrecked our flower bed," Reba replied, thrusting the crushed blooms at Daisy. "I heard a terrible racket and ran outside, and that...that creature was in my mums, tearing them out by the roots."

"But why would she do such a thing?" Daisy asked, clearly baffled by the news. Sensing her distress, Allison rose and joined them at the door, laying an arm lightly around her waist in silent comfort.

"She was probably chasing one of those precious baby rabbits who play in the yard at night," Reba replied with an injured sniff.

"Or maybe one of the squirrels we feed in the winter," Jacob coldly interjected. "It doesn't really matter. What does matter is that these flowers won the Garden Beautiful Contest this year. We put a lot of time and effort into them and expect monetary reparation for the damage."

"Oh, for—!" Meade exploded, an outburst silenced by Daisy's warning look. He clamped his mouth tightly shut and stood in silence for a moment, clearly struggling with his temper. "That cat is a stray."

"A stray?" Jacob Newman peered over Daisy's head, looking pointedly at Morgan Le Fay, who lay curled up on a quilt in the pet corner. "Looks like a pet to me."

"Well, she's not," Meade snapped. The two men glared at each other, and Allison exchanged an uneasy glance with Daisy.

"Then why don't I get rid of her for you?" Jacob retorted.

Before Meade could reply, Daisy snatched her purse off the counter and stepped between the two men. She reached inside it to draw out a well-worn billfold. "The cat *is* mine, and I'll pay for any damages. How much do I owe you?"

Obviously outraged, Meade turned on his heel and stalked from the room. Allison stared after him in astonishment, wondering why on earth he'd overreacted so badly. The cat had wrecked the garden, after all. And Daisy could certainly afford the amount Mr. Newman now requested.

Something else must be eating at him, she decided. But what? She could think of nothing, yet she still felt certain there had to be more here than met the eye. She'd seen him scratch one of Daisy's cats behind the ears, a sure sign he was reasonably fond of animals. So why did he go into orbit every time she spent a penny on them?

Should I interfere? Allison wondered, glancing toward the door through which Meade had just disappeared. Should I really jump into this friendship thing with both feet and help Daisy out by showing her meddlesome nephew the error of his ways?

The television suddenly blared from the next room. Allison heard the rapid-fire change of the channels and the agitated squeak of Daisy's platform rocker as Meade set it in motion.

Nah, she decided. Better wait until I have a few more self-defense lessons under my belt.

Chapter Seven

Wednesday began disastrously for Allison, who woke from disturbing dreams of a sexy Meade to find that Merlin had shredded a corner of her bedspread with his claws sometime in the night. At once sympathizing with the Newmans, Allison soundly scolded the cat and shooed him out of the bedroom.

She tried to boost her spirits by treating herself to a jelly doughnut at the corner bakery a short time later, but gave that up when the sticky filling landed in her lap instead of in her mouth. Clearly it was going to be "one of those days," she decided, a theory confirmed when her first appointment didn't show up and didn't bother to call and cancel.

By the time Allison finally bid adieu to her last client at five that afternoon, she fervently wished she had taken Meade up on his offer to cancel the lessons, and not just because of her bad day. Midmorning she found the handout she gave him the night before, a discovery that disturbed her to no end since he'd promised to study it.

She now doubted his desire to learn, not to mention his motives for suggesting the lessons in the first place. Did he really want to impress this L.D. person? Or was this whole knowledge exchange some clever ploy to...

To what? Allison asked herself, plopping down in one of the Queen Anne-style chairs in her office and slipping out of her too-tight shoes. Lost in speculation, she wiggled aching toes.

What could Meade possibly hope to accomplish by these one-on-one encounters if not a smoothing out of the rough spots of his personality? Allison wasn't sure, but believed she could safely rule out sex, especially after last night's fiasco. He'd had every opportunity to take advantage of her then, but hadn't, in spite of his unmistakable enjoyment of the first kisses they had shared.

Was there a difference in those kisses and last night's, which had left her so hot and bothered and Meade so cold? Allison wondered. After a moment's speculation, she told herself that it might not be the kiss at all, but the fact that she had initiated it. Meade was a man who liked to be in control. Maybe he preferred his women passive, and had been turned off by her brazen actions. That theory certainly sounded plausible to Allison, whose pride couldn't tolerate the possibility that Meade hadn't enjoyed their latest kiss as much as she had. It also explained his trying to get out of their agreement.

Why hadn't she taken him up on his offer to cancel the lessons? Allison agonized. And what now? She didn't want to discourage Meade if he truly wanted to learn, but then again, she didn't want to continue the lessons if he wasn't sincere about them. With a sigh of confusion, Allison settled back in her chair, propped her feet and closed her eyes, intending to do nothing more than rack her weary brain for what to do.

Meade found her just that way at five-thirty and stood silent at the door of her private office, his gaze resting on her face. In repose, she looked so very vulnerable, and at once he remembered Daisy's theory that her aloofness might be the result of a hurt in her past. After last night's glimpse at the passionate woman inside, Meade suspected that might actually be true. He found himself wishing he could right whatever wrong Allison had endured and melt the shell of ice surrounding her.

The depth of Meade's feelings surprised him since he hadn't even realized he cared for her beyond his intense physical attraction. He'd never felt this way about another woman and wasn't even sure what such feelings meant. He *was* sure the lessons tonight were going to be sheer torture. Just the sight of her bare feet propped on a coffee table, and the generous length of leg revealed by the slit in her skirt, had already set his pulse to racing. He positively ached with the need to touch her, to hold her.

What would she do if I kissed her awake? he wondered, immediately certain that if she responded half as enthusiastically as she had the other times their lips met, the affair he'd been thinking about all day might find a beginning tonight, right here in this office. He'd already made up his mind that such an affair would be a mistake.

Why, he couldn't seem to remember.

Meade pivoted out of her office and strode back to the reception area. Since there was still no bell on the front door, he pounded on it with his fist, then yelled, "Allison?"

"In here," she called back almost immediately. Her voice had a husky, just-waked quality, and Meade found himself wishing he could be in her bed every morning to hear it. When she appeared at her door a second later, barefoot and drowsy, he had to look away. For the second time in as many minutes, Meade questioned his decision regarding an affair with Allison. They were both single adults, after all. He wanted her, and though she probably wasn't ready to admit it yet, she wanted him, too. Why shouldn't they indulge?

I must be crazy. "Have a good day?" he blurted, rueing the moment he ever thought of this whole stupid lesson exchange.

"So-so," Allison replied with a shrug. "What about you?"

"It was all right."

"Did you review the handout on lesson one?"

"Didn't have to. I remember everything on it."

Allison crossed her arms over her chest and leaned against the doorjamb, glaring at him. "Why don't you just admit you left it in the classroom last night?"

So that was what he'd done with the darn thing.

"And if you think the classes are going to be too much for you," she continued, "why don't you admit that, too? I won't blame you for having second thoughts."

Something told Meade that maybe Allison was the one having the second thoughts. And while that solved his present dilemma by providing a way out of this mess, his considerable male pride simply couldn't tolerate her belief that the lessons were too difficult for him. "Actually, I think the classes are a breeze."

"Oh?"

"Yeah, and for your information, I really *do* remember everything on the handout."

"Prove it," Allison challenged. "Let me give you a pop quiz. If you pass, we move on. If you don't we cancel the rest of the lessons."

"All right," he agreed, suddenly inspired with a surefire means to prove he was no dummy *and* ensure that future lessons were canceled. "But on slightly different conditions. If I pass the test, you have to give me a kiss for every right answer."

Allison's jaw dropped. "You can't be serious."

"Never more so," he told her.

"But that's so . . . unprofessional."

"Who cares?"

"*I* do," Allison said, exactly the reply Meade had anticipated.

He smiled to himself, certain that she would be more than ready to call everything quits after he got through obliterating that professionalism she held in such high esteem. As for his own, well, he'd be prepared this time. Surely that would make a difference. "Aw, come on. I probably won't get any of them right anyway."

He had a point, Allison acknowledged, shamefully pleased by his offbeat suggestion now that she'd gotten over the initial shock of it. From all appearances Meade hadn't found their kiss so offensive, after all, and maybe wasn't in the least bothered by the fact that she'd initiated it. Why not make use of a delightful—if dangerous—way to find out for sure?

"You're on," she impulsively replied, certain she could control herself this time. It would only be one little kiss, after all. Two, tops. Allison walked to the classroom, followed by Meade. "Grab a piece of paper and a pencil and sit there. I'll ask the questions aloud. You write the answers."

He nodded and did as told, sitting at one of the student desks, his expression deadly serious. "I'm ready."

Allison stared into space for a moment, thinking, then said, "Under what circumstances does a man rise when introduced to a woman?"

Meade wrote something, frowned, erased what he'd just written and wrote something else. Allison shook her head in dismay and made note of the question on a scratch pad. So the classes were a breeze, huh? She felt just the barest pang of regret that he would probably do as badly on the test as he'd predicted. How could he help it? The lesson had been comprehensive, lasting almost an hour, and he hadn't even reviewed it.

She asked him ten questions in all, steadfastly resisting the urge to throw in a couple of really easy ones. When Meade handed her his paper, she took it to the podium to grade it. To her delight, he got the first question right and the second. He also got the third and fourth, as well as each and every one of the others.

Allison couldn't believe it. Stomach knotting with the certainty of having made a big mistake, she raised her gaze from the paper to find Meade watching her closely. What could well be a mischievous smile lifted the corners of his mustache.

She forced a bright smile of her own. "Congratulations. You passed."

"Oh?" He held out his hand for the test. "How many did I get right?"

"Several," she replied, folding the paper and stuffing it into her jacket pocket instead of giving it to him.

"How many is 'several'?" he asked, getting to his feet and striding toward her.

"More than half," she hedged, fervently wishing she had taken his advice to move the podium to the other end of the room. Freedom was too far away, and Meade was a very definite obstacle.

"How many, Allison?" he demanded, blocking the hasty escape she nonetheless attempted.

Allison met his gaze and then looked quickly away when she saw that his eyes twinkled and that smile she'd suspected was a full-blown cocky grin. Her heart began to thud against her ribs. One kiss would have been risky enough. Ten might prove fatal.

"All of them," she whispered.

"What?"

With effort, she sucked in air. With even more effort, she met his gaze. "All of them."

"Hot damn." He crooked a finger, beckoning to her. "Kiss me."

Allison took a hasty step back instead. "Look, Meade. I—"

He lunged, grabbing her by the waist, pulling her up close. "Kiss me."

She gulped and gave him a brief peck on the cheek. Then she tried to wiggle free.

"I meant on the mouth," he said, tightening his embrace.

"That wasn't part of the bargain," she argued.

"That wasn't *not* part of the bargain, either," he retorted. "So why don't we split the difference? Five anywhere you want to put them. Five anywhere I want them to go. It's my turn to pick, and I want it on the mouth."

Allison hesitated, then raised on tiptoe, placing a quick kiss full on his lips. "There," she said. "Satisfied?"

"Not yet, but we've got eight more to go," he told her. "Now it's your move."

Actually enjoying their banter a little, Allison tilted her head to one side, taking her time to make a decision. Meade growled his impatience. Unable to help herself, Allison laughed softly and reached up, framing his face with her hands, tugging him down to her level so she could kiss his eyelid. He caught his breath.

"Now it's yours," she told him.

"On the mouth."

Willingly she complied, letting her lips linger on his fractionally longer this time. Then, before he could prompt her, she kissed him again—on the earlobe. That done, she arched an eyebrow in silent questioning.

"On the mouth."

Shockingly eager to do his bidding by this time, Allison locked her hands behind his neck and raised her heels, a move that pressed her feminine curves against his rock-hard body. She traced his lips with her tongue, then teased them apart so she could explore the interior of his mouth. He moved his hand over her back in an exploration of his own, then dipped them down to mold the curve of her derriere. She ended the kiss reluctantly and only because she didn't want to miss her turn.

Tentatively she pushed the neck of his sweater down to reveal his collarbone. Ever so gently she brushed her lips over the entire length of it, lingering at the hollow of his throat.

"Aw, honey," he murmured hoarsely. "What are you doing?"

"It's called positive reinforcement," she replied, adding, "Your turn."

"On the mouth."

She claimed his lips with a hunger born of years of loneliness. He returned the kiss with punishing sweetness. A wild wave of pleasure caught, lifted and held her, even when Meade exhaled and set her away from him. "I don't know how much more of this I can stand," he said.

"Let's find out," Allison teased, secure in the knowledge that Meade was enjoying this insanity as much as she.

Boldly she caught the ribbed bottom of his sweater in her hands and raised it until his broad chest was bared to her appreciative gaze. She pressed her lips to a taut brown nipple and was rewarded for her daring by Meade's groan of appreciation. When she had lowered the sweater, she tipped her head back, waiting to find out where he wanted the tenth kiss.

"On the mouth."

Knowing this one was the last, her response was shameless, instant and total. She melted against Meade, giving him her all and reveling in his immediate reaction. He moved his mouth sensuously over hers, then trailed it across her cheek and down her neck. He eased his hands between their bodies to unbutton one button and then another of her silk blouse.

Lost in the gentleness of his touch, she let him push the garment aside. He dipped his head to place a kiss on the swell of her breast not covered by the lacy bra. Allison gasped, then exhaled slowly, waiting to see what he would do next. She desperately wished he would continue.

Suddenly realizing what she was thinking—and shocked to the bone—Allison sobered and crashed back to earth. Panting, flustered, she broke away from him and stepped back. With hands that shook noticeably, she buttoned her blouse and straightened her clothes. Then she smoothed her hair, all the while avoiding his gaze.

"Allison?"

Reluctantly she raised her eyes to meet Meade's. What is he thinking? she wondered as they exchanged a long, searching look. Anxiously she read his expression, finding only raw desire and perhaps a little wariness. To her relief, she saw no regret and certainly no disgust.

What do I say? she frantically asked herself. What do I do?

"Are you okay?" he asked, his voice husky and soft.

Okay? Not that, and probably never again. "Fine," she lied. "Just thinking maybe an *A* or a pat on the back might have been better, after all."

"Maybe," he agreed with a shrug. "But not nearly as entertaining."

Entertaining? Damn the man. Was that all she was to him? A summer diversion? Probably, she decided, heart sinking. At once she knew he would be on her mind long after he headed back to Atlanta—and much longer than she would be on his.

"I think it's time to get to work," she said, slipping past him and heading to the door. "I'll go get tonight's lesson."

Was it something I said? Meade thought, staring after her in bewilderment. For the past few minutes she had seemed so delightfully human...so approachable...so lovable. Lovable? Meade's heart stopped cold, then began to hammer wildly.

Lovable? No, not that. Anything but that. All he wanted was an affair, admittedly long-term, but nonetheless just an affair. He wasn't ready for commitment, for mortgages, for kids. All he wanted was a hot no-strings relationship he could easily end if she turned out like the other women with whom he'd been involved. Meade had an admitted knack for picking the wrong kind of female. More times than he cared to acknowledge, he'd found himself in a no-win situation, struggling to be someone he wasn't in a misbegotten attempt to please.

He would never let that happen again. Allison had already told him he wasn't her type. And though what had just happened between them seemed to contradict her words, Meade knew it was possible. Sexual attraction sometimes defied logic. And wanting someone didn't necessarily have anything to do with liking them, certainly nothing with loving them.

And though he liked Allison more with each passing day, he definitely didn't love her and never would. It was time to put all notions of forever afters right back out of his head.

Meade's lesson, held in the classroom as before, went surprisingly fast, probably because neither he nor Allison felt inclined to stray from the subject matter at hand. Only thirty minutes after they began going over the second handout, which dealt with business entertaining, they finished. An uncomfortable silence reigned for a long while before Meade noisily cleared his throat.

"I noticed you haven't put a noisemaker on the front door yet."

"I haven't had time," she replied, handing him the paper they'd just reviewed, and getting to her feet with an air of dismissal.

"No self-defense lesson tonight?"

She laughed shortly. "I think it might be better for all concerned if we just skipped it."

"A deal is a deal, Allison," he replied, the instructor in him miffed that she took such a serious subject so lightly. Not that he was eager to put his hands on her again. He wasn't. He hadn't even cooled down from their last encounter. He just wanted to be sure she could take care of herself if she ever had to.

She huffed with impatience. "All right, all right. Let's get this show on the road."

Meade complied, beginning with an overview that was full of tips anyone would find useful. Afterward, he showed Allison how she could break free if someone grabbed her from behind. He deliberately kept his distance during the demonstration, taking pains not to let his body brush against hers any more than necessary. Luckily Allison mastered the maneuver fairly quickly.

"That seems easy enough," she commented when she had done it correctly twice in a row.

"Just remember that it takes a lot of practice to get good at this," Meade brusquely cautioned. "I'm merely demonstrating principles. You develop proper technique by practice and it takes ninety hours of practice for any technique to become reflex. Do you understand?"

"Sure, sure," she responded, waving away his concerns.

Irritated by this flippant attitude from a woman he was so concerned about, Meade clasped her upper arm tightly. "I'm serious. A little knowledge is a dangerous thing. Get overconfident and you could get hurt."

Allison jerked free of his powerful grip, absently rubbing the tingling flesh. "What do you care?" she blurted, hoping to get some indication of his true feelings for her. She instantly regretted the thoughtless question, since it revealed how very much she wanted to know.

"I care plenty," he said, apparently unaware of her slipup. "I've been teaching martial arts for a long time. I know the wisdom of being prepared, and I want everyone else to be."

So that was it. He'd picked up on her lack of enthusiasm for this whole self-defense thing and she now presented a challenge to him—an "everyone else" for him to guide. Their kisses were probably nothing more than stimulating extracurricular activity. Well, Allison Kendall was a big girl now and didn't need guidance—in matters of safety or of the heart. "You can rest assured that I'll be careful. Now if that's all you planned for tonight, I'd really like to go home. I'm tired and I'm hungry."

Meade hesitated, almost as though he might argue, then nodded his agreement. "All right, then. Daisy fried a chicken this afternoon. If we hurry, we might get there before she gives it all to those damn cats."

Allison opened her mouth to chastise him for the comment, but shut it without speaking. Daisy was a big girl, too. She didn't need anyone to champion her cause, least of all Allison, who now regretted her decision to get friendly with the old woman and her nephew.

Daisy had not fed the chicken to the cats. Instead she served it for dinner along with mashed potatoes, gravy and the best fruit salad Allison had ever tasted. Though obviously bursting with questions about that night's lesson, Daisy held her peace until the three of them had almost finished eating. Then she leaned eagerly toward Allison. "Did you learn how to get out of a rear headlock?"

"Yes," Allison replied, purposefully not embellishing since she wasn't in the mood for talk. She'd just spent the whole meal trying to ignore Meade's intense stare, an exhausting undertaking. In hopes of discouraging further conversation, Allison helped herself to some more of the fruit salad and took a big bite.

"Was it hard to learn?" Daisy asked, undaunted.

"Not really," Allison mumbled around her mouthful.

"Think I could learn how to do it?" the spry senior citizen then questioned.

"Ask your nephew," Allison replied, cleverly passing the buck.

Daisy turned to him. "Well, Meade?"

"Hmm?" he murmured absently, never shifting his gaze from Allison.

"Do you think I could learn how to do it?" Daisy was frowning now, clearly distressed by the uncharacteristic reticence of her tablemates.

"How to do what?" Meade asked, finally looking her way and frowning in confusion.

"Break out of a rear headlock!" Daisy exclaimed in provocation.

Meade's eyes widened in surprise at Daisy's outburst. "Sure you can. Anyone can."

"Good. I want you to show me exactly what you've showed Allison," Daisy said. Meade went into a fit of coughing at that and grabbed his glass of ice water. With a puzzled frown, Daisy transferred her gaze from him to Allison, who hid her flaming cheeks by ducking down below the table to pet Merlin.

When Allison risked a peek at Daisy moments later, it was to find the older woman studying Meade again. To Allison's dismay, Daisy suddenly nodded as if she'd made a decision about something, smiled sweetly and changed the subject. "Oh, I almost forgot. I have an announcement to make. Morgan Le Fay is pregnant."

That got through to both Allison and Meade.

"What!" he exploded, leaping to his feet to glare down at her.

"That's right," Daisy said, unperturbed by his obvious displeasure. "I suspect she's several weeks along."

"You're already starving yourself to death trying to feed those damn cats now. Someone's got to put a stop to this insanity before it goes any further."

"Why?" Allison demanded hotly. "It's her money, her house, her cats. You two are only related by marriage, for heaven's sake. You have no right to tell her what to do."

"We may not be blood kin, but I'm all she has," he yelled.

"Children, children," Daisy exclaimed, visibly distressed. "Please don't fight."

Meade threw his hands up in exasperation, snatched up his jogging shoes lying in a corner and stomped out the back door, headed, no doubt, for the nearby park. Allison stared after him in disbelief.

"Is he actually going running?" she muttered. "At this time of night and after nagging me about walking home in the dark?"

Clearly relieved the tense moment had passed, Daisy chuckled and began to clear the table. "He says it's a great stress reliever, and God knows he's certainly stressed tonight. Besides, who in their right mind would attack a man built like that?"

"I might if he doesn't butt out of your affairs," Allison replied, reaching to help her. "Why on earth don't you just tell him off once and for all? He has no business fussing at you about those cats. Why, they have more right to live here than he does."

"Oh, but they don't," Daisy told her. "They're boarders, just like you and me."

Allison frowned. "What are you talking about?"

"This house belongs to Meade, dear. I just manage the renting of it for him."

Floored by the unexpected revelation, Allison dropped back down into her chair. "I thought you owned it."

Daisy laughed. "My husband and I shared ownership with the bank for a over a year, but then, as I've already told you, he had that stroke and went into the nursing home. He was a young man—fifty-seven—not old enough to receive his Social Security check. All our money went to pay the medical bills. Since I could no longer make the payments, Meade stepped in and bought the place. He did the remodeling Carl and I had planned and then opened up the top floor for rental. We agreed that I would live on the bottom floor free of charge and act as landlady.''

This revelation explained a lot to Allison, but not everything. ''The furniture is yours?''

''Most of it,'' Daisy replied.

''Then I still don't understand what Meade has against the cats,'' she murmured. ''Anyone can see they're very well behaved—'' She broke off, glaring at Merlin. ''Most of them, that is, and couldn't hurt the house itself.''

''Oh, he doesn't really mind the cats,'' Daisy told her. ''He's just frustrated with the fact that I spend so much money on them.'' She sighed. ''You see, I used to let him pay me a salary for my services as house manager. Then when Carl died, I started receiving his check and refused further checks from Meade. That dear nephew of mine thinks I'm neglecting my own needs to take care of all my babies.''

Allison suddenly saw the light. ''And are you?'' she asked.

''Don't be silly,'' Daisy said with an innocent smile. ''I'd never do anything like that.''

I'll bet, Allison thought, though she said nothing aloud. All was clear now and she suddenly understood Meade, who was probably just trying to keep a very cherished, very stubborn aunt well fed and healthy. Her heart went out to him.

Without another word, Allison got to her feet and made short work of clearing the table. Then she headed determinedly for the door.

''Are you going to bed already?'' Daisy asked, clearly surprised. ''It's only eight o'clock.''

''No. I'm going to find Meade,'' Allison replied. ''Much as I hate to admit it, I owe that man a big apology.''

Chapter Eight

Allison stepped out, fully intending to walk the short distance to the park and find Meade. She made it all the way to the end of Daisy's driveway before she remembered Meade's warning about muggings and his advice to use her head. She realized going through the park alone at this time of night was definitely not using her head.

Turning, Allison strode back to the house and climbed the steps onto the unlighted porch, where she plopped down in one of the old wooden rockers there. She set the chair in rapid motion with her foot, her gaze as far down the lighted street as she could see. Then she glanced at her watch, the luminescent hands telling her it was just after eight. Meade had been gone only ten minutes or so. It might be as long as an hour or even more before he returned.

With a sigh of resignation, Allison slowed the movement of the chair to a soothing rhythm. She relished the privacy of the dark and breathed deeply the blooming honeysuckle climbing up one of the posts supporting the porch roof. The sweet scent encompassed her, like the night sounds—tree frogs, crickets, a barking dog. Fireflies twinkled all over the yard, making it look like an extension of the star-studded sky above.

Relaxing, Allison let her thoughts go where they would and wasn't surprised when a vision of Meade filled her head. She smiled, thinking of what she had just learned about him. Somehow Daisy's revelations didn't surprise her. She'd already seen evidence of his loving, overprotective side.

Allison realized that these good characteristics far outweighed his bad one: trying to manage Daisy's life. She acknowledged even *that* habit probably stemmed only from caring concern. Was it logical to assume that he bullied her for the same reason? Allison thought that maybe it was, a realization that warmed her from head to toe and frightened her just a little.

There was no doubt about it, she decided. Faults and all, Meade was the stuff of which forever-after dreams were made. If one believed in that sort of thing, that is.

Allison didn't anymore. Twice rejected, forever shy had been her motto for years. This drastic means of avoiding a broken heart had resulted not so much from her marriage to Charles—a mistake for which she blamed only herself—as from the rejection of her jet-setting parents. The years of mental anguish caused by their betrayal had colored her whole outlook on life. And though she had long forgiven what they did to her self-esteem, she could not forget it. For that reason, she had decided it was *not* better to have loved and lost.

No man had tempted her to change her philosophy—until Meade Duran with his toe-tingling kisses. Suddenly she couldn't get the idea of a short, sweet and very steamy affair out of her head. She wanted Meade badly and, judging by his hot-blooded response to their kisses, he wanted her, too. Why not give in to this attraction and have an affair with him?

She would only be giving him her body, after all. Her heart would stay intact because she would enter into the relationship knowing it was only a matter of time before they parted again. There would be no unrealistic expectations, no false hopes. What better insurance could there be against a broken heart?

Allison couldn't think of any and wondered what to do now that she'd decided she wanted him. Though she was a liberated lady and fully convinced he wouldn't mind if she took the initiative, something in her couldn't quite conceive of actually doing such a thing.

On that thought, Allison looked at her watch again. Eight forty-five. Surely he would come back soon. And when he did, she would apologize for assuming the worst and then, since honesty was always the best policy, simply tell him that she wanted him.

There would be nothing to it. Nothing at all.

Another quick glance down the street revealed that Meade had just come into view and was, at that very moment, jogging under a streetlight about a block down the street. Eager to make her apologies and get the show on the road, Allison got to her feet and walked over to the edge of the porch.

Won't be long now, she thought, swiping suddenly sweaty palms down her skirt. Take a deep breath. Relax.

Relax? When she might be about to make the biggest mistake of her entire life? Suddenly assailed by serious second thoughts, Allison ducked back into the deep shadows provided by the thick honeysuckle vines.

She watched Meade lope onto Daisy's walk and take the porch steps two at a time. He paused then, obviously winded, and caught his breath before crossing slowly to the door. Oblivious to Allison, who huddled in the dark like the coward she really was, he reached out for the knob.

Realizing this might be her only chance to make an apology in private, Allison got a grip on her courage and came abruptly to life. She sprang for him, catching his arm. Meade started violently and whirled, looking for all the world as if he might be going to practice some of his self-defense techniques on her.

"It's me," Allison gasped, belatedly realizing the folly of approaching a black belt from behind *and* in the dark.

"Damn!" he exploded, leaping back a step. "What in the hell are you doing out here?"

"I—I need to speak with you," she stammered, what little courage she'd mustered now totally demolished. All thoughts of affairs and propositions promptly vanished into the night.

Panting and visibly shaken, Meade walked over to the rail lining the porch and looked out over the lawn. She heard his deep inhalations and waited patiently for him to recover. A whole minute passed before he spoke. "What about?"

"I had a little talk with Daisy," Allison said, getting right to the point. "She explained why you're so concerned about her finances, and it seems I owe you an apology. I had no idea you owned this house. I thought it was hers."

"Yeah, well, it would be if she weren't so damn stubborn," he muttered, collapsing into one of the rockers.

Allison sat down in the chair next to it. "I'm not sure stubborn is the right word," she commented softly. "She's more 'independent,' like me."

"Independent or stubborn, the bottom line is the same," he replied. "She won't let me give her the house or the rent it brings in, won't take a salary for managing it and spends every damn penny of her Social Security check on those stupid cats."

"She needs those cats," Allison argued. "They're all she's got."

"She's got me."

Allison laughed shortly. "For two weeks every summer. Big fat deal."

That hit home—hard. Meade squirmed, then counter-attacked. "You're one to criticize. Eight whole months you've lived upstairs, and only this week have you two gotten to know each other."

"I had my reasons," Allison replied.

Meade, who couldn't see her all that well in the meager light that filtered out through the curtained windows, sensed her defensiveness.

"And just what are those?" he asked, deliberately goading her. If he'd come to any decision on his tortuous run—and he wasn't at all sure that he had—it was to find out what made Allison Kendall tick. If he had to prod her to accomplish that, he would. "Too good to socialize with the landlady? Or is it because she's a senior citizen who just might need more of your precious time than you're willing to donate?"

"How dare you say such a thing!" Allison exclaimed, leaping to her feet. She glared down at him, hands on her hips. "For your information, I owe the happiest days of my life to my grandmother, who was a senior citizen. And I'd give anything, *anything* to have her back again."

She dashed for the door, only to be halted by Meade, who had jumped up to block her path. He'd heard the be-traying crack in her voice and realized the depth of her emotion.

"I'm sorry," he blurted. "I didn't know."

Allison gulped audibly, a sound that stabbed Meade's heart. He peered through the dark at her, wincing when he spied a solitary tear making its way down her face.

"Aw, hell, Allison," he muttered, reaching to pull her into his arms. "Don't cry." She stiffened and resisted, but Meade had no intentions of setting her free. He tightened his embrace, holding her so close she had to rest her cheek on his thudding heart to breathe.

Intensely aware of him—so hot, so sweaty, so irresistible—Allison inhaled his potent masculine scent. So this is heaven, she thought, relaxing, relishing the closeness, thinking of that affair again. Eternity passed before Meade loosened his hold on her and stepped back. He smiled and brushed a tear off her cheek with his thumb. "Want to sit out here for a while before we go in?"

Allison nodded. They returned to their rockers and sat in companionable silence for several long moments before Meade spoke again.

"I owe Daisy for the happiest days of my life," he said. "I was pretty much of a mess when I got to the States. My dad had just died, Mom had sold our home.... Anyway, I didn't want to leave Australia. Thought me and my big brothers could handle the ranch. Maybe we could've, maybe not. I don't know. I do know it took me years to forgive my mother for not giving it a try, for uprooting me, for taking me away from the grandparents and cousins I loved."

"I'll bet it *was* hard to adjust," Allison murmured, her heart aching for the rebellious young boy Meade described.

"It was pure hell," he admitted. "And that's what I gave my mother. She did her best to make me happy, worked hard so I'd have every opportunity." He shook his head. "My brothers made the transition fine and actually seemed to like that tiny, low-rent apartment where we lived. I hated it, though, and if it hadn't been for Daisy living next door, I probably would have run away."

"Is that where the cookies and milk came in?" Allison asked.

Meade chuckled. "Yeah. Her husband, my mom's Uncle Carl, was the one who got us into the apartment complex. I didn't really get to know her, however, until I broke her kitchen window with a baseball. I figured I was a goner, but she just stuck her head outside, waved and threw the ball back. A little while after that she invited me in for the cookies. I was really glad when she volunteered to watch me after school, and I even lived with her for a couple of months right after Mom remarried."

"Didn't you like your stepfather?"

"Not at first, probably because I thought Mom was betraying my dad." Meade shifted position, propping his ankle on the opposite knee and leaning back in the rocker, his hands laced behind his head. He rocked in silence for a minute. "Then Daisy explained about love and death and loving again. I finally saw the light, and my stepdad and I became good friends. Took a while, though, and I probably wouldn't have come around at all if it hadn't been for Daisy."

"Do you and your mother get along all right now?" Allison asked.

"Yeah, and Daisy had a lot to do with that, too."

"No wonder you feel so responsible for her."

"I do for a fact," Meade said. He reached out, capturing a strand of her hair and tugging playfully on it to hide his emotion. "Enough about me. Now it's your turn to talk. Tell me about yourself."

Allison shrugged. "What do you want to know?"

"Tell me about your grandmother," he prompted softly.

"My grandmother was a very special lady. At sixty-five, she took pity on a toddler no one else wanted and gave her shelter and love."

"You?" Allison could hear the shock in his voice.

"Me. We lived together until I was thirteen, when she died of a heart attack."

"Must be tough to lose your mom, dad *and* grandmother so young," Meade commented, trying to imagine life without his family. "How did your folks die?"

"My parents aren't dead," Allison told him, her voice flat. "They're living in a château in the south of France."

Meade's jaw dropped.

"I haven't seen them since they came back for Gran's funeral," she continued. "They stayed just long enough to put me in a boarding school and didn't make it back for my wedding."

"Wedding?" Meade blurted in horror, tensing all over. It had never occurred to him she might not be free. "I thought you *weren't* married."

"Divorced," Allison told him. "The man I thought would save me preferred the thrills of the stock market to the thrills of wedded bliss." She laughed shortly. "I donated a whole year of my life to Charles before I realized he would never leave that 'mistress' some people call Wall Street. But I don't blame him. He was that way when I married him. I should have known better than to think I could change him."

"He must be an idiot," Meade muttered under his breath.

"What?"

"Nothing." Meade searched his brain for something—anything—he could say to comfort her. No words came. Finally faced with the truth of Allison's painful past, he felt helpless to deal with it.

He suddenly understood her fierce need for independence, her solitary life-style. She had relied on herself for so many years she didn't know there was another, better way. Meade wondered how he could possibly convince her that life could be wonderful if shared with a warm, supportive family and a loving husband.

Loving husband?

Holy mackerel! And he'd just gotten used to the idea of a sizzling, long-term affair. Hadn't experience shown him that he wasn't the sort of man who could attract, much less *hold*, a woman of her caliber? Of course it had, and a few lessons in the social graces weren't going to work any forever-after kind of miracle.

Oddly depressed by the realization that they might never share their lives, Meade dragged his thoughts back to the present with difficulty. He reached out to take Allison's hand, and gave it a squeeze meant to show his sympathy for what she had endured.

Allison took that to mean he pitied her, something she could not tolerate. Easing her fingers free of his, she pretended to slap at a mosquito. She then got to her feet, mumbling, "We'd better go inside before we get eaten alive."

He stood at once and headed to the door.

"Meade?"

"Hmm?" he murmured rather absently, without stopping.

"What are you going to do about the cats?"

Meade halted at that and turned slowly until he faced her. "Nothing. They belong to Daisy."

Allison digested that in startled silence and then smiled her satisfaction. It looked as though she had finally gotten through. That pleased her immensely, but she knew there was still another area of concern. "And what are you going to do about Daisy?"

"What can I do?" Meade retorted with obvious frustration. "She won't take my money or listen to my advice. In another week I'll be back in Atlanta, hopefully beginning work on my wellness centers. I'll be too far away to keep an eye on her."

"Maybe there's a better way," Allison told him, acknowledging the reality of his problem with an understanding nod. "Give me a minute to think on it."

Thoughtfully she walked to the trellis at the other end of the porch and plucked one of the dozens of roses adorning it. She put the bloom to her nose automatically, not really smelling the sweet fragrance. Her thoughts were on Meade and Daisy.

More than a little independent herself, Allison could well sympathize with her landlady's predicament. Daisy battled the same two foes faced by most senior citizens across the nation—loneliness and low income. She was luckier than some, of course, and had a roof over her head, but she still had to make sacrifices to make ends meet.

Who could blame her for not wanting to rely on others for financial aid? And who could blame her if she chose the companionship of her pets over new clothes or a square meal? It was her right, after all, and she had her pride.

And it was Meade's right, if not duty, to worry about her. Was there a solution to this problem? Allison wondered. Could she, herself, possibly be it? Allison knew she could, and so very easily. All she had to do was set herself up as a guardian of sorts. She could watch over Daisy and maintain contact with Meade, something she desperately wanted to do.

But was she ready for that kind of friendship? For the love? Allison thought of her quantum leap to emotional recovery the past week and realized she just might be. That leap could surely be credited to Meade, who had given her a not-so-gentle shove from behind. And no matter what happened or didn't happen between the two of them in the future, she owed him a tremendous debt.

He had made her feel again.

"What if I find homes for all the kittens and maybe even one or two of the others?" Allison impulsively asked, walking back to join Meade. "And what if I promised to keep an eye on Daisy and call if she needed you?"

Meade eyed her warily. "You'd do that?"

"I would."

"Sure you know what you're getting into?"

"I'm sure."

Still his troubled gaze lingered on her face, as though he couldn't quite believe his ears.

"I really do mean it," she said.

At her words, Meade's face split into a wide grin. He reached out, pulling Allison into his arms and murmuring, "Thanks," into the top of her head. She accepted the hug for what it was—a platonic, spontaneous expression of his gratitude.

A millisecond later, however, Allison revised her opinion of the embrace. Pressed tightly against Meade's solid form, she couldn't help but notice his not-so-platonic reaction to it. Her own body responded to that knowledge exactly as Mother Nature had intended it should. Burning inside, she tipped her head back to collect the kiss she knew he had waiting.

His mouth covered hers, at first tender, then as demanding as his hands, which began to caress her back and hips. His touch fanned the fire already raging in Allison, and she reveled in the sweet agony.

Now, the romantic in her prompted. *Tell him that you want him.*

But the words stuck in her throat, and seconds stretched to minutes before Meade ended the kiss. He tangled his fingers in Allison's hair and held her immobile against his thudding heart, his chin resting lightly on the top of her head. Every shuddering breath told her how badly he wanted her.

And still she could not speak.

What is wrong with me? she agonized, though deep inside she knew. An old fear had her in its grip—fear resulting from years of rejection by those she loved. And while she didn't love Meade, she certainly cared for him. That meant her heart had already become involved, and *that* meant he had the power to hurt her.

It was time to slow down. No, it was time to stop. No more hugs. No more kisses. And definitely no more of this foolishness about affairs. Allison Marie Kendall might be on the road to emotional recovery, but she was, by no means, there yet.

Slowly Meade released her and let his arms fall to his sides. Now certain she'd be a fool to say what was on her mind, Allison deliberately let her golden opportunity slip by. She shivered in the night air, suddenly bereft of his body heat and her newfound confidence.

"Cold?" Meade asked.

She shook her head. "Not really. Must be someone walking over my grave."

"Don't even say such a thing in jest," he said. "I need you alive and well."

"You do?" she blurted, filled with joy in spite of every determination not to be.

Dead silence followed. Then Meade said, "Sure I do. How else am I going to keep up with Daisy after I get back to Atlanta?"

Cut to the quick by his honest reply, Allison realized just how right she'd been about his ability to hurt her. Thank goodness she'd used her head. Then she walked to the door.

"Allison, wait." Meade caught up with her in two strides. "I, uh, didn't mean that like it sounded."

"I know you didn't," she told him, forcing a reassuring smile.

Obviously relieved, he smiled back. "Before we go in, I'd like to know how on earth you plan to get rid of all the kittens."

"I have a surefire method I learned from my next-door neighbor back when I was just a kid," Allison told him. "Her cat had kittens all the time. We just put them in a box, carried them to the entrance of the nearest zoo and dangled them in front of every child going in."

"Why the zoo?"

"What better place to find animal lovers?"

Meade chuckled. "And that actually worked?"

"It sure did," she said, adding, "Of course the free cat food probably helped."

"Free cat food?" He was laughing now.

"Yes. A can for every taker."

"Oh, Allison," he exclaimed. "You're such a jewel."

"What's that supposed to mean?"

"That you're a treasure," he told her. "Sparkling, rare, priceless."

Meade reached out, brushing his fingers over her cheek. Allison felt his tender touch clear to the marrow and suddenly realized that all the good intentions in the world might not be enough to save her from Meade. Their gazes locked. He swayed toward her.

Bright light flooded the porch.

"Oh, it's only you two," Daisy said, peeking out the door at the two of them, now standing several feet apart. "No wonder Merlin was having such a fit to get out."

Way to go, Merlin, Allison thought.

With a sigh of pure relief, Allison scooped up her furry savior and darted inside.

Chapter Nine

Thursday turned out to be the kind of day that made Allison's job worthwhile. Each and every client arrived on time and showed improvement, and even at five that afternoon she still bubbled with enthusiasm and energy. Unwilling to relinquish her good mood, Allison prayed that Meade would show up on time tonight and behave himself.

Doing the sensible thing last night hadn't changed the fact that she still wanted Meade today. And though backtracking to friendship would not be easy, especially without his cooperation, it still had to be done.

Things started out well enough; he actually arrived at the office a good fifteen minutes early. Allison was quite pleased by his dedication until she realized the reason for it—he wanted to allow time for another pop quiz. It took willpower she didn't know she possessed to refuse his charming suggestion.

Though Meade seemed to take her decision in good humor, his pout told her he wasn't at all pleased, and she spied his puzzled frown more than once during her very businesslike review of the handout on telephone etiquette.

When the lesson finally ended, Meade brightened visibly and volunteered to teach her how to escape if she were jumped and wrestled to the floor. Hiding her red-hot reaction to the very idea, Allison calmly declined, choosing instead to learn how to break out of a nice, safe wrist grab. She told him she was just too tired for anything more strenuous.

Wired would have been a better word, of course, but Allison had no intentions of letting Meade know that. Typical male that he was, he would surely take advantage of the knowledge, and she would surely find herself "jumped" and loving every minute of it.

"I think I've got the hang of it now," Allison announced some twenty minutes after Meade began demonstrating proper technique. Silently she congratulated herself on managing yet again to avoid incidental body contact and still free her wrist from his powerful hold. She rubbed the tender flesh of her arm, red from his grip.

"I think you have, too," he said. He glanced at his watch. "And it's only seven-thirty. Why don't we go ahead and work on that horizontal escape?"

Horizontal escape, my foot, Allison thought, edging away from him. If they ever found themselves horizontal, there would be no escape and she knew it. "I think I'll pass. Why don't we just go on home instead? I promised Daisy I'd make a couple of pies for her big dinner tomorrow night."

"Damn. I'd forgotten about that dinner," Meade muttered, following her as she straightened the classroom and headed to her private office. "I said I'd demonstrate a few self-defense techniques to those ladies, didn't I?"

"That's what I hear," Allison said, hiding her smile at the dismay in his voice.

"Lord, I dread it."

"Why on earth? I thought you loved to do that sort of thing."

"Oh, I won't mind the demonstration," he told her. "It's the dinner after it that makes me nervous. What if I spill the drink or slurp my soup?"

"Don't be ridiculous. You've just completed comprehensive courses in etiquette, for heaven's sake. And your lesson on business entertaining covered table manners. You are definitely fit for public consumption."

"All the same, I think I'll do my thing and then split, pies or no."

"Oh, no, you don't," Allison exclaimed, suddenly inspired. "That dinner is part of your final exam."

"What the hell are you talking about?" he demanded, eyes wide with alarm.

"I can't give you a passing grade until you survive Friday night," she teased, adding, "Besides, if you live through dinner with ten—"

"Ten!"

"*Ten* little old ladies, your Saturday appointment could only be a piece of cake."

He looked a little queasy but finally managed a thoughtful nod. "Much as I hate to admit it, you do have a point," he said. Then he grinned, obviously inspired himself. "And speaking of finals, would you like to hear what yours is going to be?"

"I wait with bated breath," Allison murmured dryly as she reached in her desk drawer for her purse. Stashed inside it was the "graduation" gift she'd spotted on her lunch hour and impulsively purchased for her "friend." To-gether the two of them walked to the exit, turning off lights as they went.

"You have to be my assistant during the demonstra-tion," Meade said when they reached the door, reaching out to flip off the last switch. A blanket of darkness cov-ered them.

"But I've only had three lessons," Allison argued, smoothly flipping it on again. She realized with a start that Meade had closed the distance between them and was now mere inches away. Panicked, she pressed against the door.

"That's three more than Daisy and her friends have had," he reminded Allison, hitting the switch again.

Certain that friendship with Meade should not include making out in the dark, Allison immediately threw her hands up, ducking behind her clutch bag in a self-defense maneuver of her own creation. Meade, coming in for the kiss, bumped smack into it. Growling his impatience, he snatched the bag away.

"Why do I get the feeling you're avoiding me?" he asked, his gleaming eyes just visible now that her own had adjusted to the dark. Allison realized he'd planted one hand on the door above her head and now loomed over her, om-inously near.

"Because I am?"

"And why the hell is that?"

For the life of her, Allison couldn't remember. But Meade didn't wait for her reply, instead brushing his lips over hers. Then he nuzzled her neck with his bearded face.

Weakening, and clinging desperately to her determina-tion, Allison tried a diversionary tactic. "What did you do with my purse? I—I have a surprise for you in it."

Meade pulled back slightly and peered down at her through eyes narrowed in suspicion. "What kind of surprise?"

"A graduation present."

He hesitated, then released her to turn on the light. Weak with relief that her moment of crisis had passed, Allison accepted the purse he thrust at her. She extracted a box, which she handed him.

Clearly surprised, Meade took the present. He opened it quickly, smiling his delight when he pulled out a star-shaped paperweight.

"That symbolizes what kind of pupil you've been," Allison told him, determinedly widening the distance between them. "And I predict you'll soon be putting it on your very own desk at your very own wellness center."

"God, I hope you're right," he said, weighing the burnished brass in his hand. "I guess it all depends on Saturday night and L.D."

"Tell me about L.D.," Allison prompted to further distract him. She led the way outside and shut the door behind them. Then she dug for her keys in her bag.

"She was my best friend all during junior high and high school."

"She?" Allison blurted, so disconcerted that she dropped her keys with a jangle. "L.D.'s a *she*?"

"That's right," Meade told her. "Lisa Diane Crowley." He retrieved the keys and locked the door for her.

"You were best friends with a girl?"

"Uh-huh." Meade took Allison's arm. Firmly he nudged her in the direction of his car. "She lived on the other side of Daisy. We were very close, shared everything—our secrets, our fears, our dreams." He grinned. "Even our first kiss."

Well, darn.

"You know," he continued, a thoughtful smile on his handsome face. "It'll really be good to see her again."

"Uh, when did you see her last?" Allison asked oh so casually.

"A couple of years ago when I was here for one of my summer visits. Daisy and I ran into her at a restaurant. She was with her sister, Karen."

"Did she look the same?"

"Yes and no," he said. "Her hair was still blond, but she had it up some way, and she wore glasses. Looked every bit the brilliant businesswoman she is today."

Allison tried to picture Meade's old friend—dishwater-blond hair twisted up in a bun, thick, horn-rimmed glasses, man-tailored business suit. It wasn't a pretty picture, thank goodness.

"Is she married?"

"No."

"So that's why you were so anxious to hone up on your etiquette," she teased, greatly encouraged by her vision.

Meade grinned. "Actually, we're just good friends, and as for the etiquette, well, I figured it couldn't hurt. She's very much the lady. Always was." He sighed and shook his head. "I just hope she'll be willing to back my dream."

"Something tells me she will," Allison said, at once dead certain that no woman in her right mind could resist the likes of Meade Duran, especially an old-maid accountant.

"What are *you* doing here?" Allison blurted when she found Meade in her office around eleven o'clock the next morning. Past ready for a coffee break after more than an hour of working with a group of newly hired insurance salesmen, she wanted nothing more than ten minutes' peace and quiet before returning to the classroom.

"Waiting for you," Meade replied, unfolding his considerable frame to rise from the dainty chair in which he sat. "I was in the neighborhood. Thought I'd drop by to see if you'd tightened security yet."

"I haven't had time," she replied rather impatiently. Sometimes, or actually more often than that, Meade reminded her of a dog with a bone: gnawing, gnawing, gnawing. Today she was in no mood to be chewed on, most likely because her class wasn't going as well as usual. Allison, who'd taught etiquette to employees of this Memphis-based company several times and always enjoyed the experience, blamed today's problems on a particularly obnoxious student. Cocky as the devil himself, he had a smart comeback for every point she tried to make.

On top of that, he'd had his eye on Allison from the moment she entered the room, and she now guessed he'd like to put his hands there, too. Allison, who knew she could credit her uncharacteristic suspiciousness to Meade's recent warnings about amorous students, was ill at ease and having big trouble concentrating on her lesson plan.

"I thought as much," Meade said with a short nod. He reached behind the door, scooping up a box she hadn't noticed, and setting it on her desk with a rattle and a thump. From it, he extracted screwdrivers, a hammer, a drill, two dead-bolt locks and almost every other security device he'd suggested the night of their first lesson. "That's why I decided to take matters into my own hands." He grinned. "Where do you want me to start?"

"Nowhere," Allison snapped. The man never ceased to amaze her with his audacity. Imagine him thinking he could just waltz into her office and make changes like that without consulting her first.

"Don't tell me, let me guess. You forgot to discuss security with your landlord."

"No, I didn't," Allison retorted. "And he said I could do anything I wanted as long as he didn't have to pay for it. I have students in the classroom today, however. I can't have you disrupting things."

"I'll be quiet."

Allison glanced doubtfully at the drill and hammer on the desk, then shifted her gaze back to Meade. "Not right now."

"But someone could waltz right in here without your even being aware of it, exactly as I just did."

"No, Meade."

"But you may never get around to having it done."

"I said 'no.'"

He glared at her, then began tossing the paraphernalia back into the carton with a clatter. "Okay, okay. I'll take my locks and leave, but *you're* going to have to deal with Daisy."

"What has she got to do with this?" Allison asked.

"Who do you think sent me over here this morning?"

"She did?"

"She did." He picked up the box and turned toward the door. "Ever since I told her about those flimsy locks of yours, she's been nagging me about getting some new ones."

"She has?"

"Yeah, and she was delighted when I finally agreed to do it today." He stepped out into the reception area.

"Wait a minute," Allison called after him, recognizing what was obviously emotional blackmail, but helpless to resist it. "I have an idea."

Meade turned expectantly.

"Why don't you leave everything here and tell Daisy we'll install it sometime this weekend?"

He hesitated. "Is that a promise?"

"It's a promise."

"All right, then." He gave her a big smile and stashed the box back behind the door. Allison glanced at the clock, noting that break time would be over in a matter of seconds. The voices and laughter in the hallway told her that her students had begun to gravitate from the break room back to class. Anxious to get Meade out of the office before she got down to business again, Allison grabbed his hand and urged him through the reception area to the exit. "I hear the guys. I've got to go now. I'll see you later."

"The guys?" Meade glanced over Allison's shoulder toward the hall. "You're teaching men today?"

"Yes," she replied, reaching for the doorknob. "Until noon."

"*Old* men?"

"All ages," Allison opened the door and then turned, only to discover Meade now striding purposefully back to her office. "Where are you going?"

"I've decided I'm going to install the locks this morning, after all. You won't even know I'm here."

"But you can't—" Allison began, breaking off abruptly when she spotted her troublesome student standing in the hall, watching and listening with interest. Unwilling to make a scene, Allison joined Meade, now at her office door. "Don't...make...a...peep," she said to him softly through gritted teeth, poking a finger into the blue cotton shirt stretched over his chest. "Understand?"

He saluted sharply in reply.

And he kept his word...until he had to use the power drill and the hammer not ten minutes later. He did close the door leading to the hallway to muffle the noise as he secured her private office and the exit with sturdy dead bolts. He then hung a bell that would announce the arrival of visitors. That accomplished, he headed for the break room only to pause in the hallway, where he could hear Allison very well. Meade didn't make use of the golden opportunity to listen in on the lesson, however. He was immediately distracted by what sounded to him like a wisecracking student. Curious, he edged closer to the classroom door to try to find who the troublemaker was.

Since Allison hadn't rearranged the room yet, Meade could see most of the students without being seen by their teacher. He quickly located the loudmouth, and though wishing he could wring the young man's neck, did nothing more than glare holes in his back. Meade noted that Allison put the man in his place time and again. Apparently too stupid to realize it, he never shut up.

Meade stood in the hall a good fifteen minutes longer, listening with growing ire. He actually toyed with the idea of entering the room under the guise of working on the windows so he could give Bigmouth the evil eye, but didn't, not wanting to disrupt proceedings.

Promptly at noon, Allison ended the class. Meade heard the weariness in her voice and waited outside the door while her students filed past him on their way out. Not surprisingly, Bigmouth was not in the mass exodus. Worried, Meade entered the classroom, tools in hand. He noted that Allison's obnoxious pupil had joined her at the podium and had draped an arm over the notes she was obviously trying to gather.

"Excuse me," Meade said to Allison. "I'm just about to finish up here, but I need to ask you a couple of questions first."

"Later, sport," Bigmouth said without glancing his way. Meade set down the tools and took an ominous step toward him.

"Sorry, Mr. Crafton," Allison hastily interrupted, easing away from the podium to stand between the two men. "Business before pleasure. I'd better talk to him."

"But what about lunch?" Crafton asked.

"I don't eat lunch," she told him.

"Dinner tonight?"

"I have other plans."

"Tomorrow night?"

"She's busy then, too," Meade interjected gruffly, unable to help himself. Allison whirled to face him, obviously astonished.

"Who the hell are you?" Crafton demanded.

"Her husband," Meade retorted with another step forward. Ignoring Allison's choke of surprise, he nudged her aside to tower over the would-be suitor, who blinked in alarm and took several steps back. With an audible gulp, the man scurried around them and out the door. Meade waited until he heard the exit bell jingle. Then, quite pleased with his ploy, he turned back to Allison and grinned triumphantly.

"How dare you interfere!" she exploded, instead of congratulating him.

Meade's jaw dropped. "I wasn't interfering. I was helping."

"Helping, my foot," she retorted, eyes flashing, cheeks aflame. "That was a private conversation and you had no right to listen to it, much less to butt in. On top of that, you lied. Now that man thinks we're married."

Meade's eyes narrowed. "Are you telling me you actually wanted to go out with that turkey?"

"That's not the point," she snapped. "You had no business making that decision for me." She shook her head in disbelief. "If I didn't know better, I'd say you were jealous."

"I am, dammit."

This time, Allison's jaw dropped. Speechless with shock at Meade's unexpected admission, she didn't quite know what to say. No one had ever been jealous over her before. She wasn't sure how she felt about it other than the fact that she was oddly flattered. Her anger began to fade. "You are?"

"I am," he told her. "And I can't abide the thought of that jerk taking you out to dinner."

"You can't?"

"I can't."

The pitiful remains of Allison's temper vanished, replaced by a traitorously warm glow of pleasure. Ever mindful of Thursday's big plans to keep things friendly, she tried desperately to ignore what still remained of Wednesday's desire for a short, hot affair.

She tried and believed herself successful...until she heard her own mutinous lips blurt, "Do you have a better offer?"

Meade's face split into a broad grin. "Yeah," he said. "Dinner with *me*. Tomorrow night."

"But what about L.D.?"

His smile disappeared. "Aw, hell," he muttered. "I forgot all about her."

Meade had forgotten L.D. and what had to be one of the most important dinner appointments of his life? Allison couldn't believe it and changed that *oddly flattered* to *very flattered*. Recognizing this dangerous state of confusion for what it was, she suddenly panicked and wished she'd just kept her big mouth shut. She knew she was cruising for trouble...unless she got lucky, that is, and Meade didn't finish what she'd so foolishly started.

But luck wasn't with her. "How about Sunday night instead?"

"I'd love to go out with you," Allison said without hesitation, the next moment giving herself a mental kick in the pants for her weakness. "Just to celebrate your getting the loan, of course," she added.

"Right," he agreed with a brisk nod and a smile that said he wasn't fooled. At once Allison felt the full impact of his magnetism, so powerful and irresistible. Her gaze dropped to his lips, so kissably close. She wet her own with her tongue to assuage a sudden tingling, and tried to ignore vivid memories of how wonderful it felt to be mouth to mouth with Meade Duran.

Meade groaned at that action, then caught her shoulders in his hands and dipped his head to press his lips to the sensitive spot on her neck just below her ear. Allison gasped in response, so tense with wanting him she felt ready to explode.

"We can't . . . we mustn't. . . ."

"We will," he promised huskily, pulling her into a lung-crushing embrace. Allison gasped again, this time for air, a move that parted her lips. Meade took immediate advantage of her breathlessness, covering those lips with his and ravaging the interior of her mouth with his tongue.

A mass of sensation, Allison clung to him, eager for his touch. Sanity urged caution. She ignored it, only vaguely registering the sound of a bell somewhere far away from this eddy of need in which she helplessly whirled.

"Damn!" Meade exploded, abruptly releasing her. He did a little gasping of his own then and put several feet between them.

"What is it?" she asked, baffled by his sudden retreat.

"Someone's here," he said. "I heard the bell on the door."

"I have a bell on the door?"

He nodded. "You didn't hear it when that bozo left a minute ago?"

"No."

"Well, it's there, and a damn good thing. Two seconds more and we might've been . . ." His voice trailed off into a meaningful silence that grew weighty before Allison tore her gaze from his.

Making love, she thought, finishing his sentence in her head. A second later she changed that to *having sex,* which didn't sound nearly as scary to her and was certainly a better description of what had almost transpired. Allison's cheeks flamed with embarrassment at the realization of how close they'd come again.

Suddenly she thanked her lucky stars *and* that bell. Whirling, she scooped her papers off the podium, then headed to the door. But Meade stepped into her path, halting her before she reached it.

"We need to talk," he said.

"Not now," she replied. "That's probably my twelve-thirty appointment out front, and I want to get it over with so I can help Daisy with party preparations."

"Tonight, then," Meade said. "After dinner."

Allison hesitated, then nodded, even though she wasn't at all sure she was ready for such a talk. Once again she moved toward the door.

Once again, Meade halted her. "Is your client male or female?"

"Male. A newly hired supervisor at one of the factories."

"I see." He reached out, straightening the bow of her blouse with hands that trembled. Then he tugged her navy-blue jacket over her breasts and secured the single button.

When she frowned at him, he shrugged sheepishly. "It's either that or I audit the class."

Allison didn't bother to respond to that blatantly possessive comment. There simply wasn't time. Instead she acknowledged that whether she was ready or not, they *did* need to talk. Today's near miss had shown her once and for all that she couldn't backtrack to friendship unless Meade cooperated. She only hoped she could find the will and the words to persuade him.

Chapter Ten

During the short drive back to Daisy's, Meade mentally reviewed the list of errands his aunt had given when he left the house that morning. He checked them off one by one in his head, dead certain he'd forgotten something very important. Try as he might, he simply couldn't recall what it was. When he stepped onto the porch several minutes later, it was to find Daisy waiting at the door, arms outstretched to receive the bag of last-minute groceries he held.

"Did you get the locks installed?" she asked.

"Hello to you, too," Meade teased, giving rein to the good mood he'd been in since Allison agreed to their talk. His head still spun with the wonder of their latest encounter; he fully intended to approach her about their affair tonight. Together they would work out the details, not an easy feat since Daisy's feelings had to be considered.

Not that Meade really thought his aunt would object if he and Allison became involved. He didn't. Daisy seemed to have an open mind, after all. She was experienced in these things and surely understood how it was between a man and a woman. On the other hand, she was the product of another generation with a different set of mores. When—and if—he told her about the affair, he would have to break the news gently.

Though Meade didn't intend to conduct this liaison under Daisy's nose or even her roof, he really preferred that she know what was going on. He believed that would save a lot of awkwardness for Allison, not to mention guilt for himself. Something in him craved his aunt's understanding, if not her blessing.

"I'm sorry, dear," Daisy said with a little laugh. Tugging Meade down to her height, she placed a kiss right on his furry cheek. "Hello."

He grinned and straightened. "Yes, I did install the locks—two of them, at least. And a bell on the front door. We'll do the windows this weekend."

"Good." Daisy led the way into the house, heading immediately for the kitchen. Meade followed, sidestepping Guinevere just gliding in to investigate his arrival. At the kitchen door, he stopped short, his gaze encompassing the sparkling clean room.

"Holy mackerel," he muttered, eyeing the gleaming counters, clear for once of the canisters, cookie jar and plants usually cluttering them. He noted that the redemption coupons always suspended from the refrigerator by colorful magnets had all been stashed somewhere, as had the basket of plastic fruit, which had adorned the top of it for as long as he could remember.

"Are your shoes dirty?" Daisy, who now had a wet mop in her hand, questioned.

Meade glanced down past his faded jeans to scruffy loafers. "I don't think so."

"Take them off just in case," Daisy said. "And don't leave them in the hall. I'm going to run the buffer on it in just a minute."

Meade bit back a grin and did as requested. "Anything I can do to help?"

"Yes." Daisy abandoned her mop long enough to reach for a bottle of lemon oil and a rag, which she handed to him. "You can give all the furniture a drink. Be sure you get the mantel and that table and chair in the hall. After that I want you to run the vacuum. Don't forget the couch and chairs—they're covered with cat hair. Then you can—"

"Hold it, hold it," Meade exclaimed, holding up his hands to halt her and laughing good-naturedly. "One thing at a time. I'm liable to forget something."

"Don't worry. I'll remind you," Daisy assured him.

Never doubting for a moment that she would, Meade began his chores immediately. He worked slowly, with the awkward movements of a man who lived alone and saw little need to clean anything thoroughly.

Not surprisingly, he pictured his Atlanta home, a typical bachelor's apartment, which consisted of a kitchen, living room, bedroom and bath. He would definitely have to do a little housekeeping before Allison came to visit. She might be turned off by the stacks of sports magazines and unread newspapers, the piles of shoes, the dusty trophies.

Or maybe it would be easier just to move, he thought, dropping to his knees to reach the table legs. She might prefer something a little closer to town anyway, something with more windows or maybe a sliding glass door and a deck. He visualized the two of them spending their vacations together. They would sit on that deck at high noon in the summer, sipping a cold drink, grilling hamburgers. They'd eat at a patio table, sheltered from the sun by a colorful umbrella and then go inside where it was air-conditioned to make long, sweet love till the next noon.

Now that was a scenario he could appreciate.

"My, my," Daisy commented from the door, breaking into his imaginary idyll. Meade jumped guiltily and blushed, thankful she couldn't read minds. "You do that like a pro," she teased. "Does that mean you've been practicing on your own apartment?"

"Don't get your hopes up."

She laughed and shook a finger at him. "I thought not. You really should clean that place, you know."

He sat back on his heels. "Actually, I think I'll just move to a bigger apartment."

"Oh?" Her bright eyes took on additional sparkle. "Why would you need a bigger apartment?"

"Because I'm a big man," he told her.

"And if you don't move? That place *is* a mess, you know."

"I'll hire a housekeeper."

"A wife would be more fun," Daisy suggested, running her finger over the freshly polished surface and then peering at it like a sergeant doing inspection.

"Are you suggesting I get married just so I'll have someone to clean my apartment?" Meade asked. "Why, the liberated ladies of this fine city would tar and feather you for such a thought."

Daisy shrugged away his teasing. "Actually, I was thinking a wife might make you toe the line and clean up after yourself."

"I think I'd rather find myself a housekeeper," Meade retorted dryly.

Daisy sighed. "I thought as much. And I so wanted to spoil a precious little great-great before I died."

"You're nowhere near ready for the pearly gates," Meade told her. "And as for those little great-greats, you've already got six courtesy of my big brothers. How many do you want, for God's sake?"

"One more will do, if it's yours," Daisy replied with a pout. "I really want to hold *your* baby in my arms."

"You will," he promised. "Someday."

"Someday, someday." Daisy shook her head. "You're wasting the best days of your life. Why, at your age, I'd been married twenty years."

"Times have changed," Meade reminded her as he carefully polished the other table leg.

"They sure have and it's a crying shame. Why, marriage is going to become obsolete before long. These days it's nothing for a man and woman to live together without benefit of clergy. And most of the time the only thing they have in common is the hots for each other."

Meade nearly swallowed his tongue. So much for open minds. "Just a minute, Daisy," he said, fumbling through his own for words to explain his motives for wanting an affair with Allison. It wasn't easy, probably because he didn't know what they were. "That may be true in some cases, but definitely not 'most of the time.' Personally, I believe there are two kinds of affairs: informal and formal. The informal kind is based on lust alone. It's a short-term fling that doesn't involve sharing anything more than a bed. At this point in my life, I'm not in the market for one of those. Now a formal affair is quite different and involves sharing not just a bed but the roof over it. I believe there's merit to that kind of relationship and I might even indulge, myself, one of these days."

Daisy arched an eyebrow at that. "What kind of merit?"

"Well," Meade said, choosing his words with care, "when two people are physically attracted to each other and

want to find out if they have more than that in common, a
live-in, no-strings arrangement is the perfect solution.''

"You mean to see if they're compatible for marriage?''
she asked.

He blanched, wondering if that was indeed what he
meant. Hadn't he already decided he wasn't the stuff of
which husbands were made? Or had he? "Well...yeah.
Divorce is costly, you know, and painful. A practice run
might save a lot of heartache.''

Daisy snorted her disdain of his theory. "Or cause it.
Frankly, I think a no-strings arrangement is a no-win arrangement. Why, the whole set-up is based on the negative
assumption that the couple is not going to make it. Why not
start out positively instead, with high hopes and the commitment that might guarantee success?''

Meade had no answer to that. He'd never before thought
about the negativeness of an affair of either kind. He
wasn't sure he wanted to think about it now, but had no
choice. Verbalizing his own feelings about affairs had suddenly made clear the reason why casual sex had never appealed to him, at least where Allison was concerned.
Apparently Meade Duran still had forever after on the
brain...and in spite of all his little talks with himself.

Why? he wondered. He and Allison barely knew each
other and they certainly weren't in love. In love? Hell,
they'd never even been out on a date. Suddenly confused
about just what he did want, Meade changed the subject.
"Shall I do the piano, too?''

"Is that all you lack?'' Daisy asked.

"Uh, actually this table is the only piece I've done.''

Snorting her exasperation, Daisy took the oil and cloth
from him. "Why don't you vacuum instead?'' she said with
a sigh, pushing him in the direction of the utility closet.
"I'll take care of the furniture.''

Meade agreed with pleasure. He needed to think and knew that the roar of that old vacuum cleaner of Daisy would make further conversation between them impossible.

"Allison, you seem like a fairly typical young woman. How do you feel about formal affairs as a prerequisite to a happy marriage?"

"Formal what?" Allison blurted, caught off guard by Daisy's question. She glanced from the spry old woman busy washing lettuce at the sink, to Meade, who made a strangling noise and disappeared to the back porch, a bulging trash bag in each hand.

"Affairs. Meade and I had an enlightening discussion about them this afternoon," Daisy replied, as if they were often the topic of cozy, aunt-nephew chats. She explained Meade's theory about the two kinds, shared *his* personal preference, then added, "Frankly, I think an affair is an affair is an affair. And they have nothing whatsoever to do with happily ever afters. I'd like to hear your opinion."

"I've never really thought about it," Allison managed to say with relative calm, considering her sweeping relief upon hearing Meade's opinion. She'd been a basket case since their encounter over five hours ago, wondering how he would react when she told him she wanted nothing more than friendship, worrying she wouldn't have the strength to resist when he argued. It now looked as though all that mental anguish had been for naught.

She'd obviously read more into Meade's kisses than he had ever intended. According to Daisy, he didn't even want an affair—informal, at least. As for the formal kind, well, Allison wasn't a bit worried about his preference for those. If there was one thing of which she was sure, it was that marriage to her had never crossed Meade's mind. How could it? They hadn't known each other a week.

Never mind that it had crossed hers in that short span of time—and more than once.

"But now that I have," Allison went on, "I think Meade has a point. I'm divorced, you know, and—"

"You're divorced?" Daisy interjected, frowning.

Allison nodded and quickly continued. "Yes, and I believe that a trial run might have saved me and my ex a big mistake."

Meade, now hiding on the back porch and listening to the exchange, grinned his delight at Allison's surprising words. She actually agreed with him. That was luck he didn't deserve but intended to use to his advantage tonight when he approached her about a *very* formal affair.

Several hours of sorting out his feelings for Allison had produced a man with a plan. There was no ignoring the truth anymore. He wanted her now; he wanted her forever. He loved her. They had a destiny. It was going to begin with that formal affair and, when they were very sure of each other, end with a wedding the likes of which Great-aunt Daisy had never seen.

"Are you saying that you'd actually consider having an affair if you thought you'd found Mr. Right?" Daisy asked.

Meade held his breath and strained his ears for Allison's answer.

"Oh, not me," Allison exclaimed.

His pent-up breath escaped in a hiss of disappointment.

"And why is that?" Daisy asked.

"I'm never getting married again."

Well, hell.

"But you're only what? Twenty-four, twenty-five?"

"Twenty-seven."

"So young," Daisy said. "And never is such a long time. Don't let one little mistake ruin your whole life."

"I'm not. It's just that some people fly better solo. I've come to realize that I'm one of them."

His spirits now in his shoelaces, Meade stomped around to announce his presence and then made his way slowly back into the kitchen. He'd heard more than enough to tell him that his big plans might have to be put on hold. He was several emotional jumps ahead of Allison, who apparently hadn't even figured out that she loved him. That complicated things.

Without a doubt he was going to have to take things much slower than he'd hoped. He was going to have to hand Allison the drum and march to her beat, something the coach in him didn't do well at all. He was a take-charge sort of guy who didn't have a patient bone in his body. Waiting on Allison to sort out her feelings for him would most likely be the most frustrating thing he'd ever done. But he would do it. By God, he would do it.

Even as the doorbell announced the arrival of Daisy's guests, Meade acknowledged that the biggest challenge of his life lay ahead this night—and it had nothing whatsoever to do with little old ladies or sit-down dinners.

"Now that I've shared some common sense safety tips," Meade said just over an hour later. "I'm going to demonstrate a few nonoffensive self-defense techniques."

"Nonoffensive?" questioned a member of his audience, which ranged in age from sixty-two right on up to a youthful eighty-five.

"That's correct," Meade replied. "I teach *defense*, not *offense*. I want to stress that the only smart thing to do in a threatening situation is run."

"You're not going to teach us how to flip our attacker on his back or catch him in a headlock?" one particularly enthusiastic member of his enraptured audience asked, obviously disappointed. Since Meade was pretty sure she was the eighty-five-year-old, he had to bite back a smile before he could reply.

"I'm afraid not. That kind of maneuver would take weeks to learn and more weeks to perfect. But I will show you some easy, equally effective moves."

"Oh, good," exclaimed another woman. "This is the part I've been waiting for. If I'd taken this class a week ago, I'd still have my bag."

Realizing the speaker must be Erma, the woman who'd had her purse snatched in the park, Meade gave her a smile of sympathy and a word of advice. "It's always wise to cooperate with a thief, even if you think you could best him. No amount of money is worth the risk of death or personal injury."

He then beckoned to Allison, who joined him in the middle of the den to face the bright-eyed senior citizens. "First, I'm going to show you ladies how to break out of a simple wrist grab. Ms. Kendall, who recently graduated from one of my self-defense classes, will assist me."

Allison nodded at them—very nervously, he thought—then faced him. Meade reached out, captured her wrist to demonstrate the escape he'd taught her just the night before. She executed the maneuver perfectly, as she did every technique he illustrated over the next hour. He noted that she relaxed visibly and gained confidence as the minilesson progressed, even to the point of letting him explain some simple releases she hadn't even learned herself. Then she helped him pair off the guests so that they could practice what they'd just learned on one another.

Once the practice session was in full swing, Meade stood back so he could watch his lady love mingle with and assist Daisy and her friends. She looked gorgeous tonight, dressed in pants and a blouse that accentuated her slender waist and long legs. Her eyes sparkled with amusement at the antics of Daisy's comrades, all of whom were every bit as lively and outspoken as their hostess.

Time and again he overheard stories of how this and that friend had a shopping bag or a purse stolen and how the speaker wished *she* had been there to save the day. Time and again, he heard Allison, who'd evidently learned her lesson well, caution his audience not to get overconfident.

After several minutes of supervising practice, Meade found himself wishing he could call a recess, kidnap his assistant to the privacy of the kitchen and plant a big kiss right on her mouth, now uptilted at the corners with a warm smile. Or better yet, why not just toss her to the floor and devour her right there? But no. These sweet little old ladies would never get over the shock.

Thank goodness he'd made it through the demonstration without embarrassing himself. There would be no more tantalizing body-brushing with Allison, at least in the presence of witnesses. Later tonight there might be a little of it, an integral strategy in his newly improvised campaign to change her mind about formal affairs.

"We still have a few minutes before dinner," Daisy said at that moment. "Would any of you like for Meade to show off some of the moves that earned him his black belt? I'm sure we could talk Allison into helping out again."

The exuberant chorus of agreement that followed the suggestion bounced off the flowered walls and knocked the wind right out of Meade's sails.

"But she hasn't been trained in anything that complicated," he exclaimed, trying to discourage them. "She could get hurt."

"I'll trust you if you promise not to use that headlock or toss me flat on my back," Allison interjected, her eyes now twinkling with pure mischief.

Meade winced at her unfortunate choice of words, knowing that was a promise he couldn't make. "I really don't think—"

"Please," Daisy interjected.

"Please," her nine companions echoed. Meade took one look at their hopeful expressions and gave in, shoulders sagging.

"Oh, all right," he said. "But just a couple. I'm past ready to sample each and every one of those wonderful-smelling dishes you ladies brought with you tonight." As expected, that comment produced proud smiles all around.

Allison caught Meade's eye across the room and winked her approval. His heart turned over in response to the intimate gesture. Sending up a prayer for control, Meade walked back to the center of the room as his audience settled in their seats again. He racked his brain for something he could show these women, something that looked difficult, was really easy and involved next to no body contact.

He could think of nothing.

By the time he did finish demonstrating the two moves upon which he finally settled, sweat beaded his brow and ran in rivulets down his neck. It didn't help him a bit when Allison blotted his face with a tissue or when she used the opportunity to whisper, "You're a sweetheart, Meade Duran, and just so you can enjoy your dinner, you've already got an *A* for the course."

Gulping, Meade managed a stiff nod. A second later, he took his bows and made haste to the kitchen and the big glass of ice water he hoped would cool him down. He grabbed a plastic cup and jerked open the freezer door.

But there was no ice.

"Holy mackerel!" Meade exploded, just as Daisy and Allison joined him. "That's what I forgot to get this afternoon—ice."

"I'll go get some," Allison said.

"No, no," he told her. "I'll go. It was on my list, after all." Silently he added, *And I need the time away.*

"All right," Daisy agreed. "But hurry. All we have to do is heat up a couple of the casseroles, whip the cream for Allison's pies and brown the rolls."

"I won't be long," he promised, already heading out into the hall. He made it all the way to his car before he realized he didn't have his keys and billfold. Muttering a curse, Meade dashed back inside to fetch them. Several minutes later, he finally settled himself behind the steering wheel of his car.

Just as he inserted the key to start the engine, the house went dark. Squeals of surprise and fear immediately emanated from the open windows, and suspecting another fuse had blown, Meade got back out of the car and made his way to the pitch-black house to help.

As he stepped into the hallway, he heard Allison's shout for calm and her promise to set things to right as quickly as possible. Then, unable to see a thing in the dark, Meade ran smack into one of the end tables he'd moved from the den earlier to clear floor space, and knocked it over with a crash. One of Daisy's ever-present cats, heaven only knew which one, yowled displeasure at the noise, a sound that raised the hairs on the back of Meade's neck. Thoroughly out of sorts and grumbling under his breath, he righted the table and stomped his way down the short hall to the kitchen, which was now strangely silent.

Meade managed two whole steps into that room before some kind of cloth was thrown over his head and what felt like all ten of his overenthusiastic pupils attacked from all sides.

"Hey!" he yelled, ducking and dodging as he struggled. "It's me!" At that exact moment, one particularly aggressive guest kicked him in the bend of the knee, an action that buckled his leg and sent him right to the floor.

When light flooded the kitchen a heartbeat later, ten mouths gasped their horror. Ten pairs of hands reached out, pulling the dishtowel off Meade's head and tugging him to his feet, while the room buzzed with the sheepish apologies of wide-eyed women.

Allison, just stepping back into the kitchen from the porch, stumbled to a halt right inside the doorway, her own eyes widening in surprise. She assessed the situation and, unable to help herself, burst into laughter.

Red-faced, Meade glared at Allison, who refused to be intimidated by his temper. In a matter of seconds a sheepish smile appeared on his face, followed almost immediately by a hearty laugh that invited everyone to share the fun. Soon the kitchen was filled with the sounds of friendship and laughter. Allison made her way into the room. Still chuckling, she and Daisy herded their guests back to the den so Meade could have breathing room and they could finish their chores.

"Are you okay?" she asked him when the three of them were alone again.

"I'll live," he muttered, bending down to rub his knee.

Allison's gaze swept over him. She took note of his twinkling brown eyes, glowing skin and broad smile. Not for the first time that night, her heart swelled with something very akin to love for this man with his grizzly bear manner and teddy-bear heart. He'd been the picture of patience tonight—not an easy task for someone of his volatile temperament. From the moment he'd begun the safety talk, he'd had each and every female in the room, herself included, right in his pocket.

But she really wanted to be in his bed, and suddenly overwhelmed by a need to be closer, Allison wrapped her arms around Meade in a hug that nearly knocked him down again. Before he could get his balance enough to hug her back, she quickly released him.

"What was that for?" he asked, darting a glance at their interested witness.

"I'm not sure," Allison replied, so thankful for that same witness. There was no telling what she might have done if they'd been alone—and to a man who'd told his aunt he wasn't interested in that sort of thing. "Maybe for being such a good sport tonight."

"He certainly has been that," Daisy said, giving Meade a hug of her own. Since she wasn't in as big a hurry as Allison, he had time to return her embrace, and did so with enthusiasm.

"Did you know Allison gave me an *A* for the course?" he asked his aunt without releasing her.

"Make that an *A plus*," Allison said.

Daisy tipped her head back so she could see more than her nephew's T-shirt. "And what did you give Allison?"

"A *C minus*," he replied.

"What!" Allison exclaimed, outraged.

"You definitely need more practice," Meade said. "I was thinking a little one-on-one might be appropriate, preferably later tonight."

While Allison sputtered her embarrassment and confusion at his bold suggestion, Daisy laughed her delight. Pushing her grinning nephew away, she got back to the

business at hand—last-minute preparations for their potluck dinner. "Did you get the ice?"

"Well, hell," Meade muttered, obviously just remembering he had a mission.

"Why don't I just go get it?" Allison asked. "You deserve to sit down somewhere and put your feet up."

"Why don't you both go?" Daisy suggested with a
guileless smile at Allison and a conspiratorial wink at her
nephew. "I can manage here."

Before Allison could refuse, Meade caught her hand and
dragged her from the kitchen.

Chapter Eleven

A quick trip to the store, a deliciously forbidden kiss in Meade's car and a potluck dinner later, Allison dried the last of Daisy's delicate china plates and stashed them in the ornate cabinet. She glanced at the wall clock, noting it was nearly midnight—high time for her to be making tracks up to her room and her bed.

But she wasn't a bit sleepy and walked to the den where Meade was busy putting the last piece of furniture back in place. Daisy, one step behind him, arranged sofa pillows, vases and photos where they belonged. Meade smiled when he saw Allison in the doorway, then sank into the recliner with a sigh of what was most likely relief.

Daisy followed suit, settling herself into her rocker. She nodded her head in the direction of the couch, plainly inviting Allison to take a load off, too. Allison did, slipping her shoes off and stretching out with her head propped on the armrest. She wiggled her tired toes, an action that broadened Meade's lazy smile.

Allison dragged her gaze from him with effort, shifting it to Daisy, who looked tired and maybe a little pale. "Are you feeling all right?" she asked her landlady.

"Fine," Daisy replied. "Though I do have a touch of indigestion. Must have been Ruth Ann's chicken salad. She insists on putting too much paprika in it."

"Is there any leftover pie?" Meade asked.

"Yes," Daisy told him. "And you're not to touch it before tomorrow night." She shook a finger at him. "I think that sweet tooth of yours is getting worse as you get older. And you're supposed to know all about eating right."

"Will you give me a break?" Meade said. "I'm on vacation. I'll get back on the raw eggs and wheat germ when I get home."

"Raw eggs and wheat germ!"

"Yeah. I make this really nutritious shake by adding milk and a little vanilla." He took one look at Daisy's horrified expression and broke off with a mischievous grin. "Want me to make you one for breakfast tomorrow? It's chock-full of vitamins."

Daisy put a hand to her mouth and gulped audibly. "No thanks."

"Allison?" he asked.

Laughing, Allison shook her head. How she enjoyed their good-natured banter and easy camaraderie. How nice to be included in the circle of their friendship. It had been years since she'd felt this close to anyone. She relished the experience and the wonderful sense of belonging that resulted from it.

She wished it would never end. But it would—and soon. In another few days Meade would be gone, taking with him

the warmth she had so foolishly let herself become ad-
dicted to this past week. She would never know how it felt
to make love with this man who was so considerate, so
caring.

And so disinterested in a casual affair. Darn him.

Unexplainable melancholy settled on Allison. Sternly she
reminded herself that she didn't want one of those affairs
anyway, that she had already decided to keep things light.

"Know what I think we should do?" Meade asked,
breaking into her midnight-blue thoughts.

"Something that involves very little energy, I hope,"
Daisy murmured.

He smiled indulgently at his aunt. "I think we should go
upstairs to Allison's place and watch *The African Queen* on
her VCR. That'll give us all a chance to wind down before
bedtime."

Daisy glanced at her watch. "For your information, my
bedtime was two hours ago and if I wind down any more,
you'll have to carry me to bed. You two go on, though."

Meade glanced at Allison. "Want to?"

Though not anxious to watch a movie at this late hour,
Allison was reluctant to be alone with her topsy-turvy
thoughts. "Why not?"

Daisy smiled at that and got to her feet. "I'm going to
bed," she told them, before placing a kiss on the top of
Meade's head. "Enjoy your movie." To Allison's surprise
and pleasure, she then gave her a kiss, too, on exactly the
same spot. A second later, she disappeared into the hall and
then her bedroom door clicked shut.

Allison shifted her gaze to Meade now getting up from
his chair. When she moved to do the same, he stopped her
with a shake of his head. Catching hold of her legs behind
the knees, he lifted them enough so that he could slide his

own underneath and sit beside her. Then he picked up her bare feet, rubbing the sole of first one and then the other with his hand.

Allison sighed her contentment with his gentle ministrations. "That's heavenly," she murmured. "But if you're really serious about that movie, we'd better get started on it."

"To be perfectly honest, I'm not that eager to watch it."

"You aren't?"

"No. I'd rather use the time alone to have our talk."

So he still wanted to talk. About what, Allison couldn't imagine, since an affair, the topic she'd thought he had in mind, was definitely out. Or was it? Had he deliberately misled his aunt by feeding her all that malarkey about formal and informal affairs? Allison's heart leaped with joy at the very idea. Then she got a grip on herself. If Meade Duran had been lying to his aunt and was really interested in such, Allison Kendall was in trouble. Big trouble. "Um, down here?"

Meade glanced around the room, his gaze resting first on Merlin, curled up, as usual, near Allison, then on Guinevere, Lancelot and Morgan Le Fay, fighting over a ball of twine near the fireplace. "Too many spies. Let's go upstairs."

Allison hesitated, then swung her feet to the floor and stood. Together they walked to the stairs.

"What kind of music do you like?" Meade asked, catching her arm to halt her ascent.

"Soft rock," she replied, wondering why he wanted to know.

"Wait here. I've got a couple of tapes I think you'll enjoy." Meade made a side trip, returning moments later with two audiocassette tapes. Then together they climbed the stairs to Allison's apartment.

Once there, Meade motioned her to the love seat before making a beeline to her stereo. In seconds the muted sounds of Allison's favorite song, "Friends and Lovers," filled the air. After turning on a table lamp and turning off the overhead light, Meade joined her on the love seat. She smiled, hoping that expression would cover up her sudden nervousness.

As always, Meade's presence was electric, charging the air, *over*charging her senses. Allison risked a glance at him, and was rewarded for her efforts by his sexy smile, which did amazing things to her pulse. What's going on here? she suddenly wondered, taking note of the soft lights, romantic music. What is he up to? As afraid of her own unpredictable desires as she was of his, Allison edged away.

"Are you frightened of me?" he asked, his voice low.

"Of course not," she lied.

"Then why are you hugging the armrest?"

"Am I? I didn't realize." She scooted back a scant inch. "There. Better?"

"Hell, no," he said, reaching out to pull her not only closer, but practically into his lap. Allison stiffened in surprise. "Relax," he then said, turning her slightly so he could knead the knotted muscles in her neck and shoulders. That action reminded her of the foot massage mere minutes before and increased her suspicion that Meade Duran had more than conversation on his mind this night.

Allison's suspicions were confirmed when Meade bent forward to place his lips where his thumbs had been seconds before. She bolted right off the cushion.

"I thought you wanted to talk," she exclaimed, embarrassingly breathless, each and every hormone in her body ready and begging to burst into flame.

He sighed his exasperation with her. "I do, dammit. But you're so tense I doubt you'll even hear what I have to say."

"And kissing the back of my neck is supposed to help me relax?"

"It'd sure work on me," he said, grinning.

With a shuddering gasp, Allison made her way to the chair, which was a safe distance from Meade. "There. Now I'm relaxed. Talk."

Meade's smile faded. "Actually," he said, quite seriously. "I have a few questions to ask—important questions."

"All right," she replied, eyeing him warily.

"I like you," Meade then said. "A lot. I want to know how you feel about me."

"I like you a lot, too," Allison replied. Though not sure where he was going with this, she figured that was a safe enough admission.

Meade grinned. "That's great. That's really great." He took a deep breath and continued. "I think I'd be safe in calling the two of us friends. What do you think?"

"I'd certainly call us friends," Allison told him, somewhat encouraged by the conversation thus far. Maybe this wasn't going to be so terrible, after all. Maybe her desire for Meade had colored her conception of their encounters. She was inexperienced in casual flirtations, after all, while he was most likely a pro. It wasn't inconceivable she had read more into them than Meade ever intended and, therefore, been mistaken about his motives for this talk.

Allison thought back to the moment Meade had suggested it in the first place. As she recalled, he'd just tried to steal a kiss. Maybe her evasive tactics that night had hurt his feelings or threatened his male ego in some way. Maybe all he sought now was a little reassurance that he was desirable.

"Good. Next question. Do you believe friends should be honest with one another?"

"By all means," Allison said. Certain she knew where he was headed, she could even guess what his next question would be, and was more than willing to be honest and admit that she found him a very desirable man.

"That's wonderful." Meade stood, slipping out of his shoes and reaching out both hands to her. "Want to dance?"

Allison blinked her surprise at the question, which wasn't at all the one she'd been expecting.

"What's the matter?" he asked. "Think I don't know how?"

"No, of course not," she replied, getting hastily to her feet. If he needed to prove to her that he could dance, then dance they would, right here in her apartment with bare feet and taped music. "I just didn't want to wake Daisy."

"We're going to move real slow," he promised, putting his arms around her.

A little perplexed by their "talk," Allison kept her distance at first. In seconds, however, the throbbing beat of the ballad encompassed and soothed her. She sighed, and, as though sensing her mellowing mood, Meade pulled her closer. Allison never thought of resisting; instead she melted against him to rest her cheek on his shoulder.

Meade danced with the grace of a natural athlete. She followed his lead effortlessly, lost in the haunting lyrics about a man and woman who believed they could be friends *and* lovers.

Is that possible? Allison wondered as the music died. Could she and Meade be both to each other? In the silence before the next song, she stood immobile in his arms, wishing with all her heart that could be so.

She wanted to spend every moment of the week they had left together just as they were now—heart to heart. And though Meade had said he wasn't into short-term relationships at this point in his life, something deep inside her believed she could change his mind.

But did she really want to change it? He'd definitely be leaving next weekend and could easily take her heart with him. Were a few glorious moments in his bed worth the risk? Maybe, Allison decided, just as another love song began.

Meade swayed to the drugging beat of the music, taking her with him on another sensual journey. He held her so tightly and brushed his lips over her forehead. Allison, who ached to feel those lips pressed against hers, suddenly realized that a love affair with Meade would be an experience well worth any risk to her heart.

Besides, she told herself, there might not be that much risk involved. She had both eyes wide open, after all. She knew they did *not* love each other and could even predict when their bittersweet ending would be.

She was in control.

Their short, oh-so-sweet affair would be nothing like her miserable marriage or even one of those live-in arrangements Meade preferred. Allison smiled to herself, satisfied she had finally come to the right decision regarding Meade. This time she would *not* back down. Now all she had to do was find the perfect moment to approach him.

"Allison?" His whisper caressed her cheek.

"Hmm?"

"I have another question for you."

Guessing he was actually going to ask the one she'd anticipated several minutes ago, Allison tipped her head back so she could meet his gaze. The uncertainty in Meade's eyes seemed to confirm her theory. Ready to erase his insecurities forever, she said, "I have one for you, too. Mind if I go first?"

Meade hesitated, reluctant to give up the floor when things were going so well. He was carefully working his way up to *the* big question, and so far Allison had given him the right answer every time. He hoped she would answer it correctly, too, and say yes to a formal affair. Though that kind of relationship wasn't all that he wanted from her, he knew it was a necessary step toward his ultimate goal—marriage.

Never mind that Allison had said she wasn't interested in that sort of thing. Her kiss, her touch, her body language, told a different story. Meade was sure he could change her mind, if he was patient and did it in phases.

"I really think my question will answer yours," she added softly, breaking into his thoughts.

"Then ask it," Meade told her.

Allison stopped dancing and eased free of his embrace to walk to the love seat. She patted the cushion, smiling an invitation. Bemused, Meade sat next to her.

"This afternoon Daisy told me your theory about the two kinds of affairs. She said you weren't into casual relationships—I believe you call them informal affairs—at this point in your life. Is that right?"

"That's right," he said with a slow nod. Frowning, he added, "Was that your question?"

Allison laughed. "No. My question is would you consider changing your mind?"

Meade tensed, not daring to believe his ears. "That depends."

"On what?" she asked.

"On who wanted me to change my mind, why she wanted me to and how she went about convincing me to do it."

"I see." Allison leaned closer. "What if I told you *I* wanted to change your mind? What if my reason was desire for you?"

So much for moving real slow. "Kiss me, Allison."

"Where?" she teased, sagging against him when he reached for her.

"You have to ask?"

Apparently she didn't. Even as Meade lifted her onto his lap, her mouth found his in a mind-shattering kiss that did wonders for his enthusiasm about a casual affair. He realized he could probably suffer through one, after all, especially in light of its importance to their eventual forever after.

He dragged his lips from hers, trailing them across her cheek in search of her earlobe and that little shiver she always gave when he kissed the spot right under it.

"No," she breathed. "I'm convincing *you*, remember?"

He grinned. "Convince away."

She did. Oh, how she did—with a kiss so sweet, a caress so tender. In two heartbeats, Meade found himself bare chested. In four, he stretched out, trying to make room for them both on the tiny love seat.

But in five, Allison rolled away, getting to her feet with a huff of exasperation. After snatching a couple of sofa pillows and tossing them onto the oriental rug, she sank down on it and beckoned Meade to join her.

He did, quickly losing the ability to count heartbeats and even the will to try as his pulse—and hers—accelerated beyond measure. Lying flat on his back, Meade relished the experience of being teased, tasted and touched by Allison, who lay sprawled over him. Finally, when he could stand his passive role no longer, he rolled over to reverse their positions and managed to loosen one button of her blouse before she caught his hand in hers.

"Let me," she murmured. Slowly, her eyes never leaving his, Allison unbuttoned each and every button, then unclasped the bra she'd exposed to Meade's heated gaze. Just as slowly, she reached up, lacing her fingers behind his neck, tugging his face and lips to hers.

He kissed her deeply, letting his tongue explore the sweet interior of her mouth even as his hands explored the precious treasure she had revealed to him. With a groan, he dragged his lips from hers, trailing them downward to the dusky peak of one full breast.

Allison shuddered in response and moaned, a sound that threatened to shatter Meade's fragile control. How he wanted her. It was clear she wanted him, too. His confidence soared, and he began to wonder if all his careful plotting, all his big plans to work up to marriage, had been unnecessary. A few glorious hours in each other's arms might be all it would take to make her realize how she felt about him.

But this was not the time or place to make love to Allison. They needed to be alone, uninhibited by fear of discovery and feelings of guilt. He would take his time then, thoroughly erasing each and every one of her bad memories. He would lay to rest what remained of yesterday's fears so she could give him her tomorrows.

"Ah, honey, I love you," he murmured, caught up in his fantasy. "And I love what you're doing to me, but I don't think I'd better show you how much. At least, not now, with Daisy right downstairs. I have a lot of respect for that dear woman. I wouldn't want to hurt her."

Rigid with shock, Allison barely heard what he said. Love? Had he actually said *love*? The huge knot of dread in her stomach told her he certainly had.

But did he mean it? she then wondered. Or had the words been spoken carelessly in passion? She had to know.

"You're right, of course," Allison said, struggling to rid herself of his weight so she could sit up. When he moved to accommodate her, she clutched the front of her blouse together. "And I don't want to hurt your aunt, either. It's just that we're running out of time. You leave next weekend, you know, and then we might never see each other again."

He flinched as though she'd hit him. "Don't be ridiculous," he blurted rather loudly. "Of course we'll see each other again."

"Shh," Allison said, putting a finger to his lips. She lowered her own voice. "We might not. You're going to be very caught up in your wellness centers. I'll be busy with Etiquette, Etc."

Meade got to his feet and stood in silence for a moment, face flushed, eyes never leaving her. "What are you saying to me, Allison?"

"Nothing you didn't already know," she snapped, getting to hers, as well. "I was very up front about what I wanted from you. And I thought you understood."

"Well, I didn't," he retorted. "But I'm beginning to. Correct me if I'm wrong. You want me tonight and maybe another time or two, but only if I'm good in bed and you don't have to go out in public with me. Right?"

Allison winced at his sarcasm. "No! That's not at all what I meant," she exclaimed, baffled. Something had gone very wrong. She had no idea what.

"The hell you didn't. Lovely as your body is, Allison, I don't want it if your heart's not in it. I love you. I want to marry you."

"Marry me?" She could barely breathe.

"Marry you," he said, adding, "As in churches, preachers, rings and honeymoons."

"But we can't get married. I don't love you back and even if I did, I'd never be foolish enough to promise forever."

"Look me in the eye and say that," he challenged, catching her chin in a bruising grip. Allison had no choice but to meet his gaze.

"I...don't...love...you," she said, purposefully enunciating each word with care so there would be no mistake this time.

Dead silence followed her words while Meade searched her expression. Desperate to end this foolishness she should never have started, Allison met his gaze square on and revealed her barren heart to his examination.

"I don't know if you're lying," he said after a moment's silence. "Or if you really don't know the truth. I do know that you love me. I can see it in your eyes."

"You're imagining things," she exclaimed in exasperation, twisting free.

"I see fear there, too," he said as though she'd never spoken. "And that tells me this whole mix-up is my fault. You've had a painful past, I know that. And I really meant to work up to this proposal gradually so you would have as much time as you needed to get used to the idea of loving again. As usual, I blew it. I'm not a patient man. I can learn to be, though, if you'll give me another chance."

"But I—"

His mouth smothered the rest of her denial and sent it right out of Allison's mind. His arms held her prisoner to her passions. And though she tried to be strong, tried to resist, she couldn't and willingly parted her lips to his probing tongue. Long minutes later, he pulled away with a shuddering breath, holding her tightly against his thudding heart for a moment before he released her.

"How many other men have you kissed like that?" he asked.

"None," she admitted, weak-kneed, panting for air.

"What does that tell you?"

"It tells me I've been celibate too long," Allison replied, deliberately goading him. What they had between them was sex, not love. She was sure of it. Somehow she had to make him see the truth.

"It tells me something different," he said. "It tells me you love me and that there is a forever waiting for us."

"Look," she said, pivoting to pace the room. "You're confusing lust with love."

"I'm thirty-nine years old, Allison," he retorted, grabbing her arm to halt her march. "I know the difference. I love you. *You love me.*"

His confidence confused Allison, who suddenly found herself wondering if he could be right, after all. She certainly wanted him as she had no other man. She cared for him even more. How tempted she was to try to believe what he believed, to accept with hope what he offered.

"I need to think," she blurted, jerking her arm free and walking over to the chair to plop down in it. She put her fingers to her temples, trying to massage away the jabbing pain of her uncertainty.

"Take your time," Meade told her. "I'll never rush you again." He reached for his shirt, tugging it over his head and arms. Then he strode to the door and opened it, pausing before he exited. His eyes glistened with what could only be tears and, touched by the depth of his emotion, Allison had to blink back her own. "Sweet dreams, honey, and please, *please* let them be about me."

As Meade left the room, Merlin entered it, darting to Allison's chair and lap. She greeted the cat absently, then set him aside to spend the next hour pacing and thinking about the words Meade had said to her. He really believed she loved him. Now alone with a clear head, empty arms and an aching heart, Allison wondered if he might not be right.

"Okay," she said, nudging Merlin aside to plop down in the chair again. "Say I really do love him. Say he really loves me. What, then?"

Marriage seemed so very drastic, especially after all those years of convincing herself she wasn't meant for that institution. Nevertheless, Allison rashly let long-buried dreams of weddings, mortgages and children resurface. How wonderful those things sounded now, she realized, especially knowing Meade might be there to share them with her.

"But forever is such a long time," she wailed to the green-eyed feline. Was it realistic to hope that two people could promise that to each other and actually follow through?

She honestly doubted it was.

In desperation, Allison weighed her options. It seemed there were two: never loving at all, or risk loving and losing. She reminded herself that if she never loved at all, she would spend the rest of her life alone and lonely. After finally getting used to the joys of companionship again, Allison simply couldn't bear the thought.

That left option two: risking her heart. With luck she and Meade would love forever, happy to the end. But if the worst did happen and they parted, she would, at least, have had precious moments with him. Hungering for those moments, Allison began to understand that the same losses that made her doubt the reality of forever might also have made her strong enough to risk her heart on it again.

She was a survivor.

With a sigh of joy, Allison willingly changed her philosophy, finally admitting to herself that there were times when it *was* better to have loved. Now was definitely one of those times. She blinked back the tears of relief that stung her eyes and threatened to spill, then rose to head for the man who could make her every dream come true.

Allison came to her senses two steps from the door. She glanced at her watch; it was two-thirty in the morning. She could hardly descend on Meade at this hour. Better to wait until morning, which was long, lonesome hours away. Sighing now with impatience, she whirled to return to her chair just as someone banged on the door.

"Allison! Wake up."

Recognizing Meade's voice and the urgency in it, Allison threw open the door.

"Daisy's sick," Meade stated without preamble, already turning to head back downstairs. "I've called an ambulance."

"What's wrong with her?" Allison called to his retreating figure.

"Chest pains," he threw back over his shoulder.

"Oh, my God." It was happening to her again. Her heart jumped to her throat and all thoughts of forever afters were forgotten.

Chapter Twelve

The next half hour was a blur of wailing sirens, flashing lights and paramedics. Allison functioned mechanically, assisting when asked, doing as told, lost in memories of a night long ago when another ambulance transported another loved one to another emergency room. By the time Allison and Meade arrived at the hospital, she was numb with shock.

Meade ignored her of necessity, caught up in the details of emergency-room admission. When he returned to the waiting area after providing a clerk with Daisy's medical history and her financial status, he found Allison huddled in a chair in the corner of the vast room, staring blankly at nothing. Meade noted her ashen complexion, sagging shoulders, haunted eyes.

"Damn," he muttered softly, suddenly remembering her grandmother. Quickly he took the seat next to her. "The doctor is with Daisy now," he said, patting her hand. "One of the nurses told me she's doing as well as can be expected. We'll get another report as soon as they know something definite."

Allison nodded but said nothing.

"Don't worry," he then said. Awkwardly he lay an arm across her shoulders. "Everything will be all right."

"How do you know that?" she demanded, shaking off his touch. "The same way you know you'll love me forever? Give me a break, Meade."

Recognizing that helplessness and frustration made Allison lash out at him, Meade said nothing. He reached for her again, only to be pushed away when she got to her feet to move to another chair. Helpless to prevent her retreat into herself, Meade sat in silence, anxiously watching her every move for the next half hour.

Allison felt his heavy stare. And though she knew her questions had been unfair and probably hurt him at a time when he needed her, she could not bring herself to take them back. Cold, harsh reality had her in its grip, squeezing hope from her heart so that only pain and fear remained. In her mind, she was a teenager again, waiting alone in a room such as this one. The memories were not dulled by the hands of time and showed Allison all too clearly that she had deceived herself.

The rewards of giving your heart never outweighed the risks. It was *not* better to have loved and lost.

"Mr. Duran?"

Meade leaped from the chair. "Yes?"

"I'm Jack Brewer, Daisy's doctor. Your aunt is going to be fine."

Meade closed his eyes and swallowed, obviously struggling for composure. Touched, Allison forgot her own worries and went to him. She threw her arms around his waist in a hard hug. He returned the embrace, burying his face in her hair. Long moments passed before he released her, cleared his throat and spoke to the doctor again.

"Is it her heart?" Meade asked.

"No. Daisy's heart is probably healthier than mine. It was a recurrence of an old hiatus hernia she's had under control for years. The symptoms are very similar to those of a heart attack."

"Thank God," Meade murmured. "Can we take her home now?"

"Sure," the doctor replied. "But make her take it easy for a few days—" he grinned "—if you can."

All three of them were back home by six that morning. Meade sent Daisy to bed with orders to stay there and take the medicine the doctor had given her. Obviously basking in her nephew's attention, Daisy meekly promised.

Moments later, Meade made his way to the kitchen for the cup of coffee he hoped would restore him to a functional level. He found Allison waiting, a steaming mug in hand. She passed it to him when he stepped into the room. "I thought you might be needing this."

"Thanks," he murmured, lifting Arthur off the chair so he could take a seat at the table. Smiling, he pulled out a chair for Allison.

But she did not join him there. "Meade, we need to talk."

Suspecting he might not want to hear what she had to say, Meade shook his head. "Not now. I'm not up to it. Besides, I've got to get some sleep. My appointment with L.D. is tonight, you know."

"I do know."

"Will you stay here with Daisy while I'm gone?"

"Of course I will."

Meade studied her face. She looked tired, he thought, and maybe a little anxious, an expression that seemed to confirm his worst fears. Allison had already reached her decision about their future together, and it was not the one he'd been counting on. At that realization, depression settled over Meade. The events of the night caught up with him in a rush, and suddenly he felt bone weary. He pushed the coffee away, untasted. "We'll talk when I get back tonight, okay?"

"Okay." She nodded, giving him a ghost of a smile.

Sick at heart, unable to stand another moment in the company of this woman he wanted so very badly but might never have, Meade stood and left the room.

"Is something wrong, dear?"

Allison cringed at the question, which Daisy had already asked twice before in a different form.

"Not a thing," she lied yet again, glancing up at the clock on the mantel. It was already ten-thirty. Meade had been gone more than four hours. For the umpteenth time she wished he would hurry up and come home so she could escape Daisy's watchful eye, tell him her decision and get a start on what would undoubtedly be a painful withdrawal from her addiction to his love.

"Well, you're awfully quiet," Daisy commented from where she sat in her rocker, needlework in hand. "Worried about Meade?"

"Um, yes," Allison said, taking the easy way out. She wasn't really, though. Meade had gained enough finesse for ten men. Allison never doubted for a moment he would pull off the dinner *and* get his loan.

"Don't be," the silver-haired woman said. "I'm positive he'll get the loan. He's known L.D. for years, and just between you and me, I think she's always been a little in love with him."

Allison arched an eyebrow. "Really?"

"Uh-huh. They were inseparable when they were teenagers and even in college. When she got married, they lost touch."

"But Meade told me she wasn't married," Allison said, frowning.

"She isn't now. But she was—to Gardner McNair."

Allison's jaw dropped. "The playboy automobile magnate?"

"That's right. I believe they stayed together three or four years before she saw the light. It was a nasty divorce. No wonder she took her maiden name back."

Allison digested that information in stunned silence, reluctantly modifying her mental image of Lisa Diane Crowley, who must be something special if she'd nabbed a man like Gardner McNair. "Do you, by any chance, have a recent picture of her?"

"You know, I believe I do. Seems like I took one when we ran into her and her sister at a restaurant a couple of years ago. They came over for coffee after their meal and we had such a nice chat. Can you reach that scrapbook over there?"

Allison retrieved a thick, clothbound album from under an end table. Daisy set her needlework aside, then reached for the album and opened it about midway through. Allison joined her friend, dropping to her knees and resting her elbows on the armrest.

"Oh, look," Daisy murmured. "Here's a picture of Meade when he was two years old. Wasn't he adorable?"

Still is, Allison thought, but aloud she murmured, "Uh-huh."

"And here are his brothers. Not a normal-size male in the bunch, is there?"

"No." Allison held on to her patience with difficulty. She didn't want to see pictures of Meade or his brothers. She wanted to see L.D., who obviously wasn't the homely spinster she'd imagined and who was, at this very moment, being wined and dined by the man she loved.

"Now here's a shot of my dear husband, Carl. Handsome, wasn't he?"

"Yes," Allison replied through gritted teeth.

"The woman beside him is Meade's mother. Meade doesn't favor her a bit, does he?"

"No."

"Now let's see what's on the next page," Daisy said. Mentally sighing her resignation, Allison dropped back on her heels and rested her chin on the doily-draped armrest. She figured she might as well get comfortable. Daisy was not going to be rushed.

Together, at a snail's pace, they viewed the photographs Daisy had accumulated through the years. There were countless shots not only of Meade, his brothers and Carl, but sundry cats, cousins and renters, as well. It was all this renter could do not to snatch the album.

"Here she is," Daisy exclaimed when Allison least expected it.

Eagerly she straightened up, her eyes searching the page for the plain Jane she so desperately hoped to find.

"This woman?" Allison asked, laying a finger on a possible candidate.

"Actually, I believe that's her sister, Karen. I'm pretty sure *this* is L.D."

Allison looked where she pointed—and nearly died. Blond, buxom, drop-dead gorgeous, this woman was every woman's nightmare. And Meade was out with her! Worse, he was trying to borrow money. Allison could just imagine the terms of negotiation. Her heart, the one she wasn't going to give Meade, twisted with what could only be jealousy.

"Quite a looker, isn't she?" Daisy commented softly.

"Yeah," Allison replied, getting slowly to her feet. Shoulders slumped with dejection, she walked back to the couch and sank down.

Daisy bubbled with laughter. "Why, I do believe you're jealous. I told Meade he didn't have a thing to worry about."

"You what?"

"Told Meade he didn't have anything to worry about. That you really loved him but were just afraid to admit it."

"You actually said that to him?"

Daisy grinned. "I most certainly did."

"When?" Allison demanded.

"This very afternoon," Daisy replied, "when he told me the whole sad tale. That, if nothing else, ought to clue you as to how desperate he is."

Allison got to her feet at Daisy's words, embarrassed, yet relieved that she knew the truth. Restlessly she moved about the room, picking up this and that vase and knickknack. Her companion said nothing, merely watching her agitated movements and shaking her head slowly from side to side.

Finally, when the silence grew weighty, Daisy spoke. "Want to talk about it?"

"No. Yes." Allison sighed. "I just don't know."

"Sometimes talking out a problem helps put it in perspective," Daisy suggested.

Knowing the truth of that, Allison walked back to the couch and plunged ahead. "I'm in love with your nephew."

"I know you are."

"And he's in love with me."

"I know that, too. What I don't know is the problem."

"The problem is he wants to get married. I'm no teenager with stars in her eyes and a dream in her pocket, Daisy. I know the facts of life. It's unrealistic to believe a man and woman can fall in love and stay that way forever. I don't want to love and lose again."

"Is that all that's bothering you?"

"Is that all?"

Daisy smiled at her. "In the first place, you're wrong about loving forever, dear, and I have the proof. I fell in love with Carl Rinehart when I was eighteen years old and I still love that man today. That's fifty-seven years, so far, and I expect to love him till I die, hopefully another twenty."

"Please make that thirty," Allison said, rising to give her a quick hug and then returning to her seat. "But you don't count. You're an exception to the rule."

"I'm not, either. Remember those nine women I had over here on Friday night?"

Allison nodded.

"Seven of them are still in love with *and married* to their original spouses. Now Erma—you remember the lady who got her purse snatched? She's on her second husband. She was married to her first for fifty-one years before he died, though, so I think we can count her, too."

"That comes to only eight women," Allison noted.

"Yes, well, unfortunately I can't include Bertha. You remember Bertha?" Daisy shook her head, obviously distressed.

"Oh?"

"She's just like you. Loved a man dearly but never had the guts to get married. He finally gave up on her and found someone else. She still talks about the good times they had together, and so regrets she didn't marry him."

Allison heard the censure in Daisy's voice and blushed. "I have my reasons for being cautious."

"Your husband? Your parents?"

"How'd you know about my parents?"

"Meade told me."

"Then you must understand why I'm shaky where relationships are concerned."

"I do indeed. And while I understand and sympathize, I can't help but think you're a very foolish young woman to let your past decide your future." Daisy softened her scolding with a tender smile. "May I show you a few more pictures?"

"I suppose so," Allison said, reluctantly kneeling next to the older woman's chair again.

Daisy opened the album, this time at the beginning. "This is my wedding picture."

Allison perused the photograph, a black-and-white shot of a very young Daisy and her dashing husband. "Carl *was* handsome and you were very beautiful."

"Thank you, dear. That dress belonged to my mother. That's her right there. She was camera shy, so this is the only photo I have of her. Thank goodness I talked her into posing. She was killed by a tornado less than a month after we took it."

"I'm so sorry," Allison said. Hastily she changed the subject. "Who's this precious baby?"

"That's my son, Carl, Jr. He died of pneumonia when he was only eighteen months old. I lost another child, as well, to a miscarriage."

"And then your husband to a stroke," Allison murmured, her heart aching for her friend. How minuscule her own losses seemed when compared to Daisy's. She looked with new eyes at that dear woman, seeing not the softhearted senior citizen who took in stray cats, dogs and renters, but the stouthearted woman who'd loved and lost, yet dared to love again. What a lesson there was to be learned here. "I had no idea you'd had so much sadness in your life."

"Sadness?" Daisy frowned thoughtfully. "Maybe. But I have no regrets. You can't live without love, Allison. And if you try, you will surely end up as lonely as old Bertha, without so much as a scrapbook of memories to keep you company. Meade really cares for you. Take a chance on him. I guarantee you won't be sorry."

Touched by Daisy's plea, Allison once again weighed the pros and cons of loving. This time the scales tipped love's way.

"Oh, Daisy," she exclaimed, throwing her arms around the silver-haired woman's neck. "What a dummy I've been. Thanks so much for helping me see the truth."

"You're not a dummy, but you are entirely welcome," Daisy said, hugging her back. Setting aside the album, she stood. "Now I think I heard Meade's car door a second ago. I believe that's my cue to go on to bed."

"You're actually leaving us alone in here?" Allison gasped, clutching Daisy's arm to halt her.

The older woman chuckled and eased free of her death grip. "Of course I am. You two need to work this thing out."

"But what'll I say to him?"

"Say what's in your heart."

"I'm not sure I can," Allison admitted with a nervous laugh. "Just thinking about getting married ties my tongue in a knot."

"That's understandable," Daisy said with a nod. "Life with Meade won't be easy. He's so loud—"

"But so loving," Allison reminded her.

"So overprotective."

"But so generous."

"So bossy."

"But so tenderhearted."

"So impatient."

"But such a good kisser."

"Really?"

"Oh my, yes."

Daisy smiled at that tidbit. "Then I suggest you untie that tongue of yours. You don't want some other woman to find that out, do you?"

Allison frowned at her teasing words, suddenly remembering another woman who might already know—L.D. What if she'd made Meade an offer he couldn't refuse, one that didn't have anything to do with money? And what if Meade had decided not to waste any more time on Allison Kendall with all her hang-ups?

"Good night, Daisy," Allison said quite firmly, nudging her toward the door. "We'll see you tomorrow."

Laughing heartily, Daisy disappeared into the hall with a wink and a wave.

* * *

Outside, Meade got out of his car and walked to the house with dragging steps. Undoubtedly Allison waited inside, ready and waiting to have their talk. Meade suspected he didn't want to hear what she had to say. As he reached for the front door, it swung open to reveal his smiling aunt waiting for him in the foyer.

"It's about time you got home," she scolded playfully, eyes twinkling. "How was your dinner?"

"Interminable," he said, not quite able to return that sunny smile.

"Well, I want to hear all about it," Daisy said. "But not right now. I'm bushed, and Allison's waiting in the den to talk to you. She sent me to bed so you two could have a little privacy."

"Did she?" Meade glanced down the hall, gulping his trepidation.

"Cheer up," Daisy coaxed, reaching out to frame his face with her hands. After tugging him down so she could kiss his forehead, she murmured, "Things might not be as bad as you think."

"Yeah?" Hope welled in his heart.

"Yeah. Now go on."

Meade moved to do just that, then hesitated, turning back to study his aunt through eyes narrowed speculatively. "Do I want to hear what she has to say?"

"You're the only one who has the answer to that," Daisy replied with a loving smile that encouraged him. "Good night, Meade."

"Night, Daisy," he replied automatically, his gaze down the hall. But he never moved from where he stood.

"*Good night, Meade.*" A firm push in the small of Meade's back urged him in the direction of the den. With reluctant steps, he made his way down the hall, pausing right outside the door to gather together his wits and his nonexistent self-confidence. Then, whistling tunelessly for courage, Meade entered the room. He noted that Allison was seated on the couch, Daisy's open photo album in her lap.

"Hi," she said, looking up, smiling slightly at him.

"Hi." Shedding his jacket and tie, Meade walked over to his recliner and sat down. He glanced Allison's way, trying to gauge her mood and failing miserably.

"Allison, I—"

"How was—"

Meade laughed self-consciously. "Ladies first."

She smiled. "I was just going to ask how your dinner was."

"Productive," he told her.

She caught her breath, eyes widening. "You mean you got the money?"

"I did." He waited for her squeal of pleasure, getting nothing more than a frown, which baffled him.

Allison rose from the couch and walked over to his chair, picture album in hand. She set it in his lap, then perched on his armrest. "Which one of these women is L.D.?"

Meade glanced at the picture, one he hadn't seen, and pointed to his old friend. "That's her."

The blonde. L.D. *was* the blonde. Damn. "She's very beautiful."

"If you like blondes."

"You *don't*?"

"They're all right, but I've always been partial to brunettes, myself."

"Oh, thank God," she blurted straight from the heart, unconsciously taking Daisy's advice.

Meade said nothing to that, but he grinned a broad grin that told Allison he'd picked up on her jealousy. She didn't let that bother her. It was high time to lay her feelings for him on the line. Besides, if he was going to be partners with L.D., he needed to understand up front that his wife was not only jealous but darned territorial.

"Got any particular brunette in mind?" Allison asked, closing the album and setting it on the end table.

"As a matter of fact, I do," he said, reaching out, pulling her right into his lap and embrace. His hug was a bone crusher, and Allison couldn't have escaped it if she'd tried.

Trying never crossed her mind.

"Wise choice," she breathed into his neck instead, returning the hug with abandon.

"I think so. God, I love you, Allison." His kiss was long and satisfying. She sighed with regret when he finally raised his head, sighed and laid her cheek on his thudding heart.

"I love you, too, Meade, and I want to marry you. If you still want me to, that is."

"Of course I do," he said, kissing her again to prove it. When he raised his head this time, they were both breathless and aching for more.

"I'm sorry I doubted you," Allison whispered, unbuttoning every last button on his shirt so she could push the fabric aside and kiss the pulse tap-dancing in his neck. He responded by slipping his hand under her T-shirt to cup her bare breast. She arched to his tender touch, barely managing to utter, "I never will again."

Meade pushed her shirt up to her neck, dipping his head to taste first one taut peak and then the other. "Never say never, honey," he murmured when he'd teased both thoroughly. "We've got the rest of our lives ahead of us."

"We sure do," she agreed with a wry grin. "And unless you want to start on it right here and now, I suggest you stop what you're doing."

"I guess I'd better," he agreed, though he didn't remove his hand.

"Meade?" She tried to ease away from him.

He let her go with obvious reluctance and a frustrated sigh. "How does a June first wedding sound?"

"Perfect," she said, straightening her clothes. She then rebuttoned his shirt, covering the temptation of that marvelous chest. "The sooner we get married, the happier I'll be, especially now that you're going to be partners with one of those blondes you don't prefer." She frowned. "I know I should be thrilled for you, but frankly, I wish your old friend were the other woman in that picture, or better yet, a man."

"Actually my new partner *is* a man."

Allison tensed. "What are you talking about?"

"My new partner is Sterling Wagner, L.D.'s fiancé. He's an orthopedic surgeon. She brought him along tonight because he was so intrigued by my idea when she told him about it. Then he wound up offering me the money instead of L.D. We're going to open our first center here in Memphis."

Allison finally squealed her delight, a sound that brought Merlin bounding into the room. Claws bared, he leaped at Meade.

"Damn cat!" Meade exploded, grabbing for him.

Squealing again, Allison scooped up her overprotective feline and held him out of harm's way. "Don't you dare hurt my cat. If it weren't for him, I'd never have met you."

"What are you talking about?" Meade demanded, clearly baffled.

Quickly she told him about Merlin's magic on that Saturday morning a week—or was it a lifetime?—ago.

Meade grinned when she'd finished her tale, then reached out to scratch that clever cat behind the ears.

"Way to go, Merlin!" he exclaimed. "Way to go."

* * * * *

COMING NEXT MONTH

#736 VIRGIN TERRITORY—Suzanne Carey
A Diamond Jubilee Book!
Reporter Crista O'Malley had planned to change her status as "the last virgin in Chicago." But columnist Phil Catterini was determined to protect her virtue—and his bachelorhood! Could the two go hand in hand...into virgin territory?

#737 INVITATION TO A WEDDING—Helen R. Myers
All-business Blair Lawrence was in a bind. Desperate for an escort to her brother's wedding, she invited the charming man who watered her company's plants...never expecting love to bloom.

#738 PROMISE OF MARRIAGE—Kristina Logan
After being struck by Cupid's arrow—literally—divorce attorney Barrett Fox fell hard for beautiful Kate Marlowe. But he was a true cynic.... Could she convince him of the power of love?

#739 THROUGH THICK AND THIN—Anne Peters
Store owner Daniel Morgan had always been in control—until spunky security guard Lisa Hanrahan sent him head over heels. Now he needs to convince Lisa to guard his heart—forever.

#740 CIMARRON GLORY—Pepper Adams
Book II of *Cimarron Stories*
Stubborn Glory Roberts had her heart set on lassoing the elusive Ross Forbes. But would the rugged rancher's past keep them apart?

#741 CONNAL—Diana Palmer
Long, Tall Texans
Diana Palmer's fortieth Silhouette story is a delightful comedy of errors that resulted from a forgotten night—and a forgotten marriage—as Long, Tall Texan Connal Tremayne and Pepi Mathews battle over their past...and their future.

AVAILABLE THIS MONTH

#730 BORROWED BABY
Marie Ferrarella

#731 FULL BLOOM
Karen Leabo

#732 THAT MAN NEXT DOOR
Judith Bowen

#733 HOME FIRES BURNING BRIGHT
Laurie Paige

#734 BETTER TO HAVE LOVED
Linda Varner

#735 VENUS DE MOLLY
Peggy Webb

Diana Palmer's fortieth story for Silhouette . . . chosen
as an Award of Excellence title!

CONNAL
Diana Palmer

Next month, Diana Palmer's bestselling LONG, TALL
TEXANS series continues with CONNAL. The skies
get cloudy on C. C. Tremayne's home on the range
when Penelope Mathews decides to protect him—by
marrying him!

Silhouette Romance®

A duo by Laurie Paige

There's no place like home—and Laurie Paige's delightful duo captures the heartwarming feeling in two special stories set in Arizona ranchland. Share the poignant homecomings of two lovely heroines—half sisters Lainie and Tess— as they travel on the road to romance with their rugged, handsome heroes.

A SEASON FOR HOMECOMING—Lainie and Dev's story…available in June

HOME FIRES BURNING BRIGHT—Tess and Carson's story…available now

Come home to A SEASON FOR HOMECOMING (#727) and HOME FIRES BURNING BRIGHT (#733) . . . only from Silhouette Romance!

HOME FIRES BURNING BRIGHT (#733) is available now at your favorite retail outlet. If you missed A SEASON FOR HOMECOMING (#727) or wish to order HOME FIRES BURNING BRIGHT (#733), order them by sending your name, address, zip or postal code along with a check or money order for $2.25 for each book ordered, plus 75¢ postage and handling, payable to Silhouette Reader Service to:

In the U.S.
901 Fuhrmann Blvd.
Box 1396
Buffalo, NY 14269-1396

In Canada
P.O. Box 609
Fort Erie, Ontario
L2A 5X3

Please specify book title(s) with your order.

HB-1AA

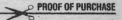